FORTUNE'S FAVORS

A CLAIRE ROLLINS COZY MYSTERY BOOK 5

J. A. WHITING

Copyright 2018 J.A. Whiting

Cover copyright 2018 Susan Coils at www.coverkicks.com

Formatting by Signifer Book Design

Proofreading by Donna Rich

This book is a work of fiction. Names, characters, places, or incidents are products of the author's imagination or are used fictitiously. Any resemblance to locales, actual events, or persons, living or dead, is entirely coincidental.

All rights reserved.

No part of this publication can be reproduced or transmitted in any form or by any means, electronic or mechanical, without permission in writing from J. A. Whiting.

To hear about new books and book sales, please sign up for my mailing list at:

www.jawhitingbooks.com

❀ Created with Vellum

For my family with love

1

"I had the strangest dream last night," thirty-five-year-old Claire Rollins said from her sitting position on the small stool as she stocked a shelf in Tony's Market and Deli.

"I have strange dreams every night. Somehow I manage to shave fifty years off my age in my dreams. Too bad that doesn't carry over into real life." Tony, in his early seventies, tall with broad shoulders, set down a carton of soup containers next to Claire. "Here's the last one, Blondie. No need to finish the stocking before you need to leave for work."

With their toenails clicking on the wood floor, Claire's two rescue Corgis trotted past her following Tony to the front of the small, Adamsburg Square market tucked into a cozy, historical neighborhood next to Boston's Beacon Hill.

"What was your dream about?" Sitting at a café table sipping coffee with retired state supreme court judge, Augustus Gunther, Tessa raised an eyebrow and gave Claire a concerned look.

"It wasn't so much what happened in it, it was the sensations that came over me." Claire moved some of the cans and boxes around on the shelf to better fit the items she was stocking. "I was making something in my kitchen and somebody pounded on my front door. It was loud and forceful and the sound of it sent chills of dread through me."

"Did you open the door in your dream?" Augustus asked. The older man wore his usual outfit of a tailored suit, perfectly pressed white shirt, and necktie. Years of dressing for court was a habit the judge would not change, even in the heat and humidity of Boston's summers.

"I didn't. I kept dreaming the same thing, over and over, all night long. It was weird. I feel like I didn't sleep at all." Claire shook her head and reached into the carton.

"Maybe someone really was knocking on your door," Tessa suggested pushing an auburn curl from her eye.

"I wondered the same thing. I did get up to check once." Claire paused with a soup can in her hand. "When I think of it, the same awful feeling rushes through me."

"I've had dreams that stay with me after rising." Augustus stirred his coffee with the slim wooden stick. "Odd how they linger sometimes. Any explanations for those kinds of dreams?" the judge asked Tessa.

In her fifties, Tony's girlfriend, Tessa, held a job in the financial district of the city, but worked part-time as a psychic, telling fortunes, employing Tarot cards, interpreting dreams, and counseling people about their pasts, presents, and futures. When she'd told Tony about her special skills, he had snorted and laughed, but when he saw she wasn't kidding, his demeanor swiftly changed and they had a long, respectful discussion about paranormal abilities.

Augustus, on the other hand, wasn't at all surprised by Tessa's news and asked about the topic as if they were talking about any usual occupation.

Tessa replied to Augustus's question. "Dreams can be a re-hashing of someone's day, they can be a way to highlight something of importance that the dreamer is overlooking, they can point to a concern the dreamer is ignoring. They need to be considered within the framework of what is going on in the person's life. Sounds, images, events don't stand for the same things in everyone's dreams. Those things can be symbolic of other things. That's why interpretation must be a careful process."

Augustus looked to Claire. "Have you had this dream repeatedly over several nights?"

"I haven't, no. Just last night." She stood, broke down the empty carton, carried it to the store room recycle bin, and then returned to sit at the café table.

Tony brought a new carafe of hot coffee to the beverage bar he'd set up on a cramped counter at the back of the store where customers could find tea, coffee, decaf coffee, sugars, and milk and cream. Three small tables had been set up for people to sit and enjoy their drinks before heading off to work.

The Corgis greeted the three people at the table for the third time that morning and then hurried into the store room and out through the propped open back door to the walled-off, grassy area behind the store where they could chase balls or rest under the small tree. The dogs stayed at Tony's store with him while Claire worked at her friend's chocolate shop in the North end.

"Those dogs have the life," Tessa smiled as she watched them scoot away.

"I'd better get a move on." Ninety-one-year-old Augustus swallowed the last of his coffee. "I'm meeting some former colleagues for a walk in the park." The man winked. "That is our code for getting together for a gossip session about the city's legal doings." The judge wished his friends a good day and walked briskly out of the store to the brick sidewalks of the square.

When some customers came in and Tony went to wait on them, Tessa looked pointedly at Claire. "What's up with this dream you had?"

Pushing her long, naturally-curly blond hair up into a loose bun, Claire asked, "What do you mean?"

"It seems to have bothered you."

"It did, but we all have nightmares from time to time."

"You didn't describe it as a nightmare. You described it as *strange* and *recurring*. A nightmare usually frightens a person," Tessa said. "Did this dream scare you?"

Claire ran her finger in small circles over the tabletop, thinking. "I was anxious, full of dread ... and sort of sad. It was as if someone needed something from me that I couldn't give them."

Tessa's eyes held the young woman's.

"What?" Claire asked. "Why are you looking at me like that?"

Tessa reached for her briefcase. "Time will tell."

With narrowed eyes, Claire said, "I really don't like it when you say that. It usually means something is about to happen and that *something* is never good."

"You've helped people several times so you could describe those situations as being good." Tessa stuffed her phone into the bag. Since moving to Boston, Claire had assisted in helping solve several city crimes.

"I just want things to be normal."

"You're special, Claire. Things that need fixing will find you." Tessa stood, gave the young woman a kind pat on the shoulder, and walked to the front of the store to give Tony a kiss before heading to her job.

All of her life, Claire's intuition had been strong, but before moving to Boston, she'd been able to brush it off as coincidence or something anyone could sense. Since her husband had died and after moving to Massachusetts, her skill had grown while living in the city and now it was nothing she could dismiss or ignore and Tessa had been a huge help in assisting Claire with acceptance that her ability was outside of normal.

With a sigh, and some worry that something might be brewing, Claire gave Tony a hug and left the store for her friend, Nicole's, chocolate shop. The walk to work took her past the gold-domed state house and the Common, through Faneuil Hall Marketplace and Christopher Columbus Park and then into the North End.

The day was sunny and pleasant with a bright, blue sky and a warm breeze occasionally coming off the ocean. After work, Claire looked forward to taking the dogs to the Common for a romp and then going for a run, hopefully with her boyfriend, Detective Ian Fuller, if he was free.

The previous evening, she and Ian, along with Nicole and her new boyfriend, went for dinner at a new restaurant and then strolled along the waterfront together. Thinking back over the enjoyable evening, Claire couldn't pinpoint anything about the get-together that might have precipitated her dream of someone knocking incessantly at her door.

Nicole met Dr. Ryan Foley at the hospital when Ian had been attacked by a killer, and the sparks flew as soon as they laid eyes on each other. Ryan had similar interests and enjoyed running, biking, swimming as well as snacking on Nicole's delicious chocolate treats.

Once when Ryan mentioned he'd better slow down on consuming the shop's tasty goods, Ian had said, "Just give up. No one can resist those sweets."

When Claire opened the door to the shop, Robby, the twenty-one-year-old, part-time co-worker, greeted her by saying, "Well, well. Look who decided to finally show up at work." He glanced at Nicole. "We don't have to do everything ourselves now that Claire decided to grace us with her presence."

Claire smiled at the talented, young, music student and kidded him, "You're welcome. Now that I'm here, the shop will run smoothly and efficiently." She took an apron from the wall hook, pulled it over her head, and brought a tray of chocolates out to the glass case.

With a chuckle, Nicole gave her friend and employee a hug. "Ignore him. He's in rare form this morning." Filling one of the coffee machines with water, she said, "We had a great time last night. Ryan fits in with all of us so well."

"He's a lot of fun," Claire nodded. "Ian and I really like him."

"So do I." A bit of pink flushed Nicole's cheeks.

"I'm so glad Ian got bashed in the head last month. Otherwise, Ryan and I never would have met."

Claire laughed. "I'll let him know how happy you are he got hurt."

Robby walked by carrying a package of napkins to fill the holders on the coffee bar. "Let's go, ladies. Save your swooning over those men of yours for later. I'm about to unlock the door to admit the hungry hoards."

"Okay, we're ready." Claire headed to the backroom for the last tray of chocolate sweets for the glass cases. Several customers entered the café as she was slipping the tray into the case and when she looked up, she saw Ian approaching the counter.

Her heart did a little flip of joy when she spotted the good-looking detective, but when she noticed his expression, an unusual feeling of dread came over her.

Just like the dread from the dream she'd had last night.

Uh, oh.

2

It was late afternoon when Claire and Ian walked the dogs along the Charles River in the fading October light of the day. The Corgis, Bear and Lady, sniffed the ground and wagged their tails at the other dogs they met on the path, and at the joggers and walkers.

When Ian arrived at the chocolate shop that morning to see Claire, she knew something was on his mind by the set of his jaw and the tightness around his eyes.

"I've been approached by someone I used to know in elementary school about a cold case," he told her.

Claire's heart sank at the words *cold case*. She and Nicole had just finished up assisting Ian on a long, involved cold case and Claire had no interest in being dragged into another one. They made arrangements to meet when her shift at the shop was over and all day, she was distracted and antsy.

"Wait and see what Ian has to say," Nicole told her. "If he asks for help, I don't think we can say no to him."

Claire would never refuse to help. She just hoped that wasn't what he wanted to discuss.

"Someone I knew in school contacted me," Ian said as they walked. The reds, oranges, and yellows of the leaves reflected in the river. "Her name is Kelly Carter Cox. We went to school together until grade two when she moved away. She heard I was a detective. I have to say I barely remembered her."

"She has a connection to a cold case?" Claire waited for Bear to finish sniffing at the base of a tree.

"Her mother," Ian said. "My parents must have shielded me pretty well from bad things because I can only recall hearing that Kelly's mother had died when we were in kindergarten."

"I'm going to guess the mother didn't die from natural causes?" Claire looked at Ian out of the corner of her eye.

"She did not. Kelly knocked on my office door this morning, early. She asked if I remembered her. I didn't until she told me her name and how she knew me. Her mother was murdered. After the murder, Kelly went to live with her grandmother, but before second grade, she left town to join her aunt's family. Turns out, the grandmother couldn't function after her daughter was killed. Kelly needed a healthy family so the aunt took her in.

"Why has she come to see you now?"

"It's been thirty years since her mother died," Ian said. "The anniversary is coming up. She said it's been eating at her that the killer was never found. She asked me if I could help."

"What did you tell her?" Claire asked as she zipped up her light jacket.

"I told her I didn't know how much time I could devote to it. I work for the city of Boston. The crime took place twenty minutes from here in Chatham Village. I know a couple of guys who work there and we get along well, but I don't think I could give much time to the case. It would have to be done in my spare time, and really, that isn't anywhere near the amount of time that would be necessary."

"What did she say to that?"

"She said she'd already spoken with the detective in Chatham Village and he would look into the case, but he'd like any help and input I could give." Ian took Claire's hand. "I know you aren't crazy about getting involved in another cold case."

Claire said, "You're right. These cases are upsetting. I have a hard time compartmentalizing. Once I'm involved, I can't stop thinking about it."

"I understand. But I have to ask you if you'd consider looking at the case notes. Would you talk to Kelly about what happened to her mother? You see things that everyone else misses. You and Nicole have a knack for uncovering details, for noticing things that the rest of us miss."

Claire sighed. Ian did not know that she had a heightened ability to sense things. Tessa called it paranormal skills, but she didn't like the term. It made her feel odd, like people would shun her and think she was strange or a kook or some such thing. Tessa did her best to convince Claire that her skills shouldn't be thought of in that way. She told Claire that some people are natural athletes or scientists or mathematicians ... and other people had the natural ability to see and feel things that others were blind to.

Although Claire knew she had to tell Ian about this side of her, and soon, she dreaded the idea. "I guess I could look at the notes."

"Would you be willing to meet with Kelly?"

"Sure. I can do that." Claire seemed to be trying to convince herself that getting involved would be a good idea.

Ian apologized. "If it's too much, I understand. It's okay if you say no. Don't feel pressured."

Claire's shoulders slumped a little. "I can't say no. If someone needs help, I can't just tell them no."

"Yes, you can. If it's too upsetting, you can absolutely say no."

"Nope. I can't." Claire gave him a half-smile and squeezed Ian's hand. "I'd like Nicole to be with me when I meet with Kelly."

"I agree," Ian said. "Nicole is great at sorting through information. Thanks for doing this. It's a huge favor to me and I appreciate it."

A little smile moved over Claire's lips. "I'm sure I'll think of a way for you to repay me."

Ian put his arm around his girlfriend and pulled her closer.

～

"I KNOW THAT CASE," Robby's blue eyes flashed with interest as he frosted the cupcakes. He, Claire, and Nicole were working late to prepare bakery items for an event the next day that Nicole had contracted for.

"How do you know it?" Claire slid a cake pan from one of the ovens and set it on the counter to cool.

"I read those internet sites about unsolved cases," Robby said. "It's a hobby of mine."

"How do you have time to go to college, practice your music, perform, and work here?" Nicole asked. "And then spend time reading over cold case sites?"

"It's relaxing."

"Reading about murders is relaxing?" Nicole turned up her nose.

"Trying to figure them out is relaxing," Robby explained. "It's something different for me to do. I'm always interacting with people or practicing or performing. Sitting at my laptop gives me some quiet time."

"So what do you know about this case?" Claire cut some brownies into squares and set them on platters.

"The mother was killed late in the evening ... in October, I think," Robby said. "The little girl was asleep in her room. The police thought the mother, what was her name?" Robby looked off across the room. "Janice, I think. Yes, that was it. Janice must have known her killer because there was no sign of forced entry."

"She opened the door to him then?" Nicole asked.

"That's what the police suspected."

"If someone rang the bell though, she might have gone to answer it and opened to see who was there," Claire surmised. "People weren't as cautious back then as they are now."

"That's true, but who would come knocking late in the evening?" Robby asked. "Wouldn't you be suspicious if someone knocked or rang your bell at that time of night?"

"First, I'd ask who was there," Claire said. "If the person said *police* or *there's a gas leak that needs to be fixed*, then I bet I would have opened the door."

"So Janice might have known the person or she was tricked by someone claiming to be an official and she opened up." Nicole poured batter into a cake pan.

"Right," Robby said. "Janice must have opened the door. There was no sign that someone broke in."

"What else do you know?" Claire questioned.

"Let's see. The little girl, Janice's daughter, went to live with relatives."

"Her name is Kelly," Claire said. "She and Ian attended kindergarten and first grade together and then Kelly moved to live with her aunt."

Robby's forehead scrunched in thought trying to recall what he'd read online about the murder. "I think a neighbor claimed to see someone going inside, but I might be mixing up details between cases I've read about."

"What kind of a house was it?" Claire asked.

"Why? What does that matter?"

"I was wondering why Kelly didn't wake up," Claire told them. "Didn't she hear a fight or an argument or people crashing around the house?"

"I don't know what the house was like." Robby sounded disappointed that he'd missed a detail.

"Did Janice and her daughter live in the house alone?" Nicole asked.

"Yes. Just the two of them."

Claire turned to face Robby. "Ian didn't mention how the woman was killed. Was she shot?"

"Stabbed to death," Robby informed her. "That detail, I didn't miss. Her throat was cut and she was stabbed multiple times."

Nicole's face looked grim. "In the morning, the little daughter came out of her room to that? To her mother dead from a stabbing? It's too terrible."

Claire stood silently thinking and after a few moments, she said quietly, "I'm not sure I want to talk to Kelly Cox."

"You can't back out now," Nicole told her friend. "The appointment is scheduled. We're seeing her tomorrow afternoon."

Ice felt like it was filling Claire's stomach. "I know. I won't cancel it, even though I'd like to."

"It will be okay. I'll be with you. It happened thirty years ago. I doubt we'll be able to point out anything the investigators overlooked. We'll meet with Kelly Cox, read the case notes, and that will be that. We'll have tried, but there won't be anything to go on."

Claire looked over at Nicole with a worried expression. "You said that last time, on the last case we worked on."

"Well." Nicole held a spatula in the air as she spoke. "Maybe this time, we won't be able to get involved."

"It worries me," Claire said. "If the killer was in his twenties when he committed the crime, he'd only be in his fifties now. He's not an old man. He could come after us."

"Don't worry, Claire," Robby kidded. "I'll protect you."

The blond baker glanced over at her young co-worker and a heavy sense of dread descended and nearly choked her.

3

"I was five years old when my mother was murdered." Kelly Carter Cox sat on her sofa across from Claire and Nicole in her home in the city of Chatham Village. The thirty-five-year-old woman had dark brown eyes and chin-length, light brown hair with some gold highlights in it. She was about five-foot, five-inches tall and carried a few extra pounds on her frame.

The home was a white, Colonial with a one-car garage and a small area of grass in the rear and was located on a tree-lined street of similar houses. Kelly worked as a math teacher in one of the city's middle schools.

"Do you remember anything about that night?" Claire asked.

Kelly leaned against the sofa back with a sigh. "I remember waking up earlier than usual. The light was just peeking in past my bedroom window's curtains. Funny, but I felt off, something felt off. I didn't know what it was, but something seemed wrong. Maybe the house was too quiet, maybe that's what made me feel uneasy."

"Can you tell us about the layout of the house?" Nicole asked.

"Sure. My mom rented a small bungalow. It had two bedrooms. Mine was right off the living room. There was a small kitchen and there was a dining area between the kitchen and living room. There was a short hallway that led to my mother's bedroom. The bathroom was off the hallway."

"What happened after you woke up?" Claire questioned. Her heart pounded like a hammer.

"I got out of bed. Usually, I pushed the curtain back a little to look outside to see if it was sunny or rainy or whatever. I didn't do that. I walked to my bedroom door. It was closed. I leaned down to look through the peephole. It was an old house. The bedroom doors had those old-fashioned locks you needed a key for. They never got locked, we didn't have the keys. There was a peephole on the doors though." Kelly let out a long breath. "I saw my mother on the living room floor."

Nicole waited a few moments before she asked the next question. "Did you open the door and leave your room?"

"I did." Kelly's voice was soft as she looked down at her hands clasped tightly together. "I went into the living room."

"Did you know your mother was dead?" Claire asked gently.

"I knew it." Kelly nodded. "There was blood all over the place."

"What did you do?"

"I looked down at her. Her body was face-down, but her head was turned to the side. Her face was turned away from me towards the sofa. I could see the side of her face. She had blood on her cheek."

"Did you stay inside?"

"No. I ran out of the house. I was in my pajamas. I ran out to the walkway. The neighbor, Mr. Adams was in his yard. He looked up when I came out. He was about to say hello to me, but then he must have seen the look on my face. His expression changed. He asked me what was wrong." Kelly paused. "I told him I thought my mother was dead."

Claire and Nicole exchanged looks of sadness, each of them thinking about the horror of that day.

"What did Mr. Adams do?"

"He called to his wife," Kelly said. "She stayed with me in the yard while Mr. Adams went inside our house. He wasn't in there for long. He came rushing out, his face was like a ghost. I went into the Adams's house with Mrs. Adams and she made me some breakfast. Mr. Adams must have called the police because they showed up while I was eating my eggs."

"How did you feel?" Claire asked.

"Confused." Kelly's forehead scrunched. "I didn't know about death at that age. I didn't understand. Part of me thought my mother would wake up. I didn't realize it was permanent. Mr. and Mrs. Adams were always nice to me. I remember him showing me a butterfly that was on his shoulder one day. We didn't touch it, we just looked at it until it flew away. I wasn't afraid or anything that morning because they were with me."

"Did someone come for you?" Nicole asked.

"My grandparents came. They didn't live far from us, maybe ten or fifteen minutes by car. My grandmother was crying and I started to cry when I saw her. My grandfather's face was serious, but I could see it in his eyes. He didn't look like he usually did. He looked afraid to move."

"You went to live with them?"

"I did. It was only for a year and a half. My grandfather got sick and my grandmother couldn't handle it, especially right after losing my mother. It was a very hard time for her. I think my grandfather's illness was triggered from the loss of his daughter. I went to live with my aunt in Hull. I stayed with them until I went to college."

"Your mother would be sixty now?" Claire asked.

"She would. It's been almost thirty years since she was killed." Kelly ran her hand over her hair.

"Why have you asked the detectives to look into the murder now?"

"I don't know exactly why," Kelly said. "It's been eating at me. Time is going by. No one has been arrested. Soon it will be too late, everyone involved will be dead. Maybe it's too late already, but I have to try. I went to my mother's grave on her birthday and I promised her I'd try to find her killer."

Claire gave the woman an understanding nod. "Thinking back on the night of the murder, did you wake up that night? Did any noise disturb your sleep?"

Kelly put her hand to the side of her face. "I've

been asked that a million times. I've asked myself that a million more. I don't remember waking up. I don't recall hearing any sounds. Maybe my mother didn't scream because she feared waking me. Would the killer have attacked me, too, if I got up and opened the door that night? Did my mother keep silent in order to protect me?"

"Who was the detective who handled the case back then?" Claire asked.

"William Boyd," Kelly said. "He was with the Chatham Village police department. He's in a nursing home now. He has dementia. He isn't able to converse at all. I don't think he knows who he is or where he is."

"Have you spoken with the police about the case?" Nicole asked.

"I talked with a detective here in town. That's how I found out about Detective Boyd being in a nursing home."

"Who did you speak with?"

"Detective Gagnon. Mike Gagnon."

"He has agreed to look into the case?"

"He was reluctant. I had to convince him. He told me there probably isn't any way to find new information and that the investigation will go nowhere. Detective Gagnon said that every now and then, a member of law enforcement takes a look at an old case, does some digging, and either decides to go forward with it or makes the decision to abandon it. He told me my mother's case has been looked at many times and that nothing new comes to light."

"But you talked him to taking another look?" Nicole asked.

"He said he'll look into it, but he can't promise anything. He talked to your detective friend, Ian Fuller, to get additional eyes on the case. And now, the two of you are here." Kelly smiled. "This is probably the most attention my mother's case has received in thirty years."

"You know that it will most likely be very difficult to find anything new?" Claire questioned. She hated the idea of disappointing Kelly. "Solving it, finding the killer, well, the odds are probably worse than trying to win a lottery. You understand that we will probably come up empty? You need to brace yourself for that."

"I know what everyone is saying about the chances of finding the killer." Kelly's lips held tight together. "I don't care what anyone says. I promised my mother. If it takes me the rest of my life, I won't give up until I have the answer."

"We'll all do the best we can," Claire said with a

serious expression. "But sometimes, the best isn't good enough." She worried that Kelly would not be able to handle a disappointing outcome.

"Has Detective Gagnon been able to get hold of the case notes and the evidence bags?" Nicole asked.

Kelly swallowed. "The items are no longer available."

"What does that mean?" Claire asked. "Why not?"

"There was a small fire several years ago in the police department building and the evidence bags associated with my mother's murder were destroyed."

Claire's heart sank. No evidence? How could Ian and Detective Gagnon work a case with no evidence? "It was destroyed? All of it?"

Kelly gave a slight nod. "It was lost in the fire."

"What did Detective Gagnon say about that?" Nicole asked.

"He said it would make things even more difficult." Kelly had a hard time forcing those words from her throat.

Claire thought that was an understatement. How could a case be investigated with no evidence?

"Despite the lost evidence," Nicole said, "Detective Gagnon is still willing to open the cold case?"

"He's asking around." Kelly nodded at the two women. "He's trying to find something, anything before he gives up on it. He's trying to find some of the people who were around back then. The officers who arrived on the scene. Some reporters or lawyers, or whoever might know things."

"What about Mr. and Mrs. Adams, your former neighbors?" Claire asked.

"They're in an assisted living facility not far from here," Kelly said. "Detective Gagnon will visit them and ask some questions."

"The case notes were lost in that fire, too?" Nicole questioned.

"Yes, they were."

Claire groaned inwardly. *This case is going to be impossible.*

4

"The evidence and case notes were lost in a fire at the police station." Claire wiped down the table across from Tessa who had dropped into the chocolate shop between clients for a quick coffee.

"So what will happen?" Tessa held her cup near her lips. "Is that the end of re-opening the case? It can't be looked at if there isn't anything to look at."

"Au contraire." Robby stopped next to Claire after delivering a latte to a customer. With a hand on his hip, he glanced from Claire to Tessa. "Aren't you going to ask me what I mean?"

"What do you mean?" Claire asked the young man.

"I told you I hang around those cold case

websites. I'll post something about the case and ask for help. You wouldn't believe how many people read those blogs and sites. Lots of amateur sleuths have been instrumental in solving cases."

"I don't know," Claire said with hesitation.

"Don't worry. It's not a bunch of kooks," Robby explained. "Well, there are some kooks, but most people just want to help. Plenty of law enforcement officers frequent the sites. It's like crowdsourcing. You ask people for help and you often get it."

"I'll text Ian about it to get his okay."

"Fine with me. He'll say *yes*, you wait and see." Robby went back to the counter to wait on some customers.

"Robby probably has a good idea." Tessa wiped her lip with her napkin. "As it stands now, you've got nothing to go on."

There was a lull in customers entering the shop and Nicole came over to talk to Tessa and Claire. "I felt so badly for that woman. Imagine opening your bedroom door and finding your mother dead on the floor outside your room." She shook her head. "Kelly Cox is probably lucky to be alive. What would have happened if she woke up when the man was attacking her mother? Would he have killed a little child, too?"

"Thankfully, that didn't happen." Tessa's eyes darkened. "How was the interview with Ms. Cox? Did she recall things from that morning?"

"She told us she didn't hear anything during the night," Nicole said.

"Kelly said she woke earlier than usual and that she peeked through the keyhole in her door before going out into the living room," Claire said. "That tells me that she sensed something was wrong. Maybe she *did* wake up during the night, heard a commotion, was afraid, and burrowed under her covers. Or she woke slightly, heard fighting, fell back to sleep, but when she woke, she remembered something from the night … maybe the noises outside her room and that's why she acted cautious by looking through the keyhole."

"That could be true." When Tessa nodded, her auburn curls bounced. "I wonder."

"What?" Nicole looked at Tessa with interest.

"I wonder if Ms. Cox has ever undergone hypnosis."

"Hypnosis?" Claire's eyes narrowed. "Isn't that just hocus-pocus?"

Tessa straightened and said to the blond young woman, "Is your ability to sense things hocus-pocus?"

Claire glanced nervously around the crowded café and slipped into a seat at Tessa's table. "Keep your voice down," she whispered.

"Does hypnosis really work?" Nicole asked.

"It can, yes," Tessa said. "Some people are more responsive to hypnosis than others, but researchers have yet to determine why that is. Hypnosis doesn't cause the subject to fall asleep nor does it make the person unconscious. On the contrary, the mind of a hypnotized person becomes hyper-focused and hyper-attentive and the subconscious is more accessible."

"You think hypnotizing Kelly Cox would help her remember things from that night?" Claire asked. "Could it bring forward some things that have been buried in her mind?"

"It's happened before," Tessa said. "I wonder if hypnosis has been tried already with Ms. Cox."

"Information from hypnosis can't be used in court, can it?" Nicole asked.

"On a very limited basis," Tessa said. "But if Ms. Cox recalls anything about that night, the police might be able to follow it up to produce some hard evidence. If all else fails, keep it in mind as a last resort."

Claire said, "Kelly's former neighbors, Mr. and

Mrs. Adams, lived next door to the house she lived in when her mother was killed. They're in their late seventies or early eighties. The detective who has agreed to look into the case will speak with them. Maybe something helpful will come out of the meeting."

Robby walked up to the table and handed Claire her phone. "Text Ian and ask him if I can post about the case on those websites."

Claire took her phone and sent the message.

In less than a minute, a reply pinged Claire's phone. After reading the text, she said, "Ian says yes, go ahead and post on those sites."

"I knew it," Robby said triumphantly and turned for the backroom. "I have my laptop in my backpack. I'll post right away explaining that the evidence and case notes are lost and if anyone knows anything about the case to please contact me."

"It can't hurt," Nicole said as she watched the young man walk away.

"Do you know anything about Kelly Cox's mother?" Tessa asked.

Claire said, "Her name was Janice Carter. She was thirty when she died. She never married Kelly's father. He died while serving overseas in the military. Kelly never met him. Janice worked as a dental hygienist and she went to school at night with the hopes of eventually becoming a nurse practitioner."

"Was she dating anyone?" Tessa questioned.

"Janice dated off and on," Nicole said, "but there wasn't anyone she was seeing on a regular basis. Kelly was told these things when she was older."

"Did she ever have a fight with anyone she was dating?" Tessa questioned. "Did anyone bother Janice. She could have stopped seeing someone who didn't care to be dropped."

"Kelly didn't know anything about that sort of thing," Nicole said. "That doesn't mean it didn't happen. Janice might not have shared that information with her parents."

"How about the neighbors?" Tessa asked. "Did suspicion fall on any of the neighbors?"

Claire shook her head. "Kelly only knew that the neighbor across the street told police he might have seen a man ring the doorbell at Janice's house the night of the murder, but it was dark and the neighbor wasn't able to describe the man. Other than that, we don't know."

Some customers opened the door and stepped in and Nicole and Claire stood up to wait on them as Tessa took the last sip of her coffee and headed back to work. "Don't give up," she encouraged the two young women. "It looks hopeless right now, but you've only taken the first steps. There's a long way to go. Fortune will smile on you and your efforts."

Later in the afternoon, Nicole, Claire, and Robby were baking in the backroom when Robby asked Claire, "How come you never told me your late husband was so much older than you?"

Claire spun around and stared. "How do you know that?"

"I looked you up on the internet."

Claire's face paled and her stomach tightened. There were things about her background that she didn't want revealed and although she'd done internet searches on her name, she'd never found any evidence of her net worth. "Why did you look me up?"

"Because you're secretive." Robby folded some eggs into a mixture.

"No, I'm not."

"You don't admit you have paranormal powers." Robby held his hand up. "Don't deny it, Clairvoyant Claire. You knew I had that audition when I never mentioned a word about it." Months ago, Claire had sensed that Robby had an important audition and without thinking, wished him well on his performance. He brought the matter up fairly frequently, but Claire always blew it off.

"Will you admit you have some sort of paranormal powers?" Robby asked and then grinned. "Don't worry, I'll still be friends with you."

Claire picked up the whisk and began to whip the mixture in her bowl. "It's rude to spy on people."

"I'll take that as a yes," Robby said without looking up. "So your late husband was a lot older than you, huh? Like what? Forty years older? Don't get angry with me. It's unusual, that's all. I wondered why you married someone so much older."

Claire stopped whisking the batter and turned to face Robby. "Because … I loved him."

Robby didn't say anything right away, but he gave Claire a sweet smile. "The best reason of all."

"Get back to work, you two," Nicole said teasingly. "And no more spying on Claire. If you want to know something, just ask her. And don't spy on me either."

"I'm making no promises." Robby spooned the batter into muffin tins. "Anyway, it's not spying, it's gathering information. It's the twenty-first century. Everyone does it."

Nicole was about to say something else when Robby's laptop dinged from across the room. He dashed over to look at his email and after a few moments, he said, "That didn't take long."

"What is it?" Wiping her hands on a dish towel, Claire walked to where Robby was standing to look over his shoulder.

"It's a reply to my request for help." Robby beamed.

"What does it say?" Nicole hurried over.

"It's from a retired police officer. He says the case was looked at several times over the years and despite not finding anything new to pursue, he and another officer took notes and compiled a report with details on the case."

"Was the report lost in the fire, too?" Claire asked.

"It was."

Claire's heart dropped.

Robby said, "But, this officer has a copy of the report in his home office."

"Where does he live?" Nicole's voice was full of excitement.

"In Chatham Village," Robby said. "The same town where Janice was murdered."

With a wide smile, Claire raised a hand and high-fived Robby and Nicole. "Fortune's favor has been sent our way."

5

Claire and Nicole pulled into the driveway of a grey Colonial home and parked near the garage. A tan dog was sleeping on the front lawn and he lifted his head momentarily, glanced at the car, and then rested his head back on his legs.

Nicole noticed the dog and said, "I guess we don't look very threatening. Either that or the dog has given up his position as house security officer."

Claire chuckled and rang the front bell. The door opened in just a few moments and a short, stout, gray-haired man greeted them with a warm smile and handshakes. "Jack Phillips. Come on in."

He led them to a screened porch off the kitchen where they took seats on comfortable chairs. "I copied the report for you. I understand Detective Gagnon is having a look into the case. I called him to be sure it was okay to let you see the report. He was surprised to hear I had it. I dropped off a copy to him at the station."

"Detective Gagnon must have been very happy to hear about the report," Claire said. "There wasn't much to go on since the evidence and case notes were destroyed."

Jack smiled broadly. "He sure was. The report was tucked away in my file cabinets down in the basement. I never expected the case to be opened again."

"We don't know if it will be re-opened," Nicole said. "It's only in the information gathering stage right now. Years have gone by since you looked into the murder. We're only doing this because the victim's daughter has requested the case be re-opened."

Jack rubbed at his chin. "The daughter must be what? Mid-thirties?"

"Kelly Cox is thirty-five," Claire said. "She works as a teacher here in town."

"She was in college when we looked through the case notes. That was about eighteen years ago. I always wondered what would become of that little girl. How does a child recover from such a thing? Not only losing her mother to violence, but finding her dead body." Jack shook his head slowly. "I'm glad to hear she has a good job. Did she marry?"

"Kelly's been married for about ten years," Claire told the retired officer. "She seems happy. Except for wanting her mother's killer to be found."

Jack's face turned serious. "Every law enforcement officer who worked on or looked into the case has done their best. When I went over the case notes years ago, I searched and searched for a shred of evidence to follow. I came up empty. I'm hoping new eyes on the information will find something. I think you two not being in law enforcement might be of benefit. Coming at the case with a different way of looking at things might prove to spark new ideas."

Claire waited for the retired officer to ask about their backgrounds and why the police brought them onboard, but when Jack didn't question them about it, she wondered how Detective Gagnon explained their participation in the investigation.

"Would you mind if we asked you a little about the case?" Nicole asked.

"Not at all. I read through the report last night to refresh my memory. I'd like to help if I can."

Nicole thanked the man. "Kelly Cox has given us

her account of the morning she found her mother on the living room floor and what happened subsequently. We know a little about Janice Carter, she had Kelly at age twenty-five, she was unmarried, she worked as a dental hygienist and was going to nursing school at night. Janice had dated now and then, but was not in a relationship. Does that all match up with what you know?"

"It does, yes. You heard there's a good chance Janice knew her killer? There was no sign of forced entry so she must have opened the door to whoever knocked."

"We heard that," Claire said. "There could be the possibility that someone knocked and claimed to be a police officer or a utility worker who might have lied about a gas leak or an electrical problem in order to gain entry."

"That's within the realm of possibility," Jack said.

"We also heard there was a neighbor who told police he might have seen a man knock at Janice's door that night? Do you know anything about that?" Claire questioned.

"Yeah. He was no help at all. Too vague, didn't see the man's face, couldn't describe what the man was wearing or how he arrived at Janice's home. No one in law enforcement was sure the neighbor saw anything. The guy might have wanted to seem important so he made up a story. Either way, he couldn't give any details so it didn't lead anywhere."

"The next-door neighbors, Mr. and Mrs. Adams, didn't hear or see anything either?" Nicole asked.

"They didn't hear a thing. They only knew that something was wrong when the little girl ran out of the house and told Mr. Adams her mother was dead."

"Did Janice have any close friends?" Claire questioned.

Jack said, "She did. Two women. One of them was going to nursing school with Janice. The other knew Janice since middle school. Neither could offer any information that could be called a lead. Time is funny, though. The passing of the years can bring an old memory to the forefront. Something triggers it, a question, a smell, a sound. When the person is in the midst of the turmoil, things can get glossed over or ignored, and then the memory wiggles its way out of the mind's depths and shows itself. And that becomes the thing that leads to finding the killer."

"I hope that happens this time," Claire nodded hopefully.

"There was another incident on the night Janice Carter was killed," Jack told them.

Adrenaline coursed through Claire's veins. "What was that?"

"There were some kids playing down at the field. It's a park and there's a baseball diamond, a couple of basketball courts, a grassy area. The kids lived a block from the field. A guy sat on a bench watching the kids play. A girl was riding her bike. Her sister and brother were shooting baskets. It got late and the kids needed to go home. The older sister and brother headed out thinking their sister had ridden her bike home. Only she hadn't. She was riding on the paved paths down by the ball field. When she got back to the basketball court and didn't see her siblings, she started to head home."

When Jack paused for a sip from his water glass, Claire leaned forward. "Did something happen to the little girl?"

Jack set his glass on the side table. "A guy was watching the kids. He was sitting on a bench drinking a soda or something. The girl rode her bike past a hedge at the edge of the field and somebody pushed her off the bike. She got up and ran, screaming. Her sister and brother weren't far away. They heard the screams and ran back. The little girl ran to them and told them a man was running after her. The sister and brother didn't see the guy around.

The kid was pretty shaken up. She was sure the man was chasing her."

"Did anyone call the police?"

"The kids' mother called to report the incident. Officers arrived and took statements, then looked around for the man, but they weren't able to locate him."

"That was the end of it?" Claire felt a rush of nervousness pulse over her skin.

"No. Later in the week, the kids were asked to go to the police station to take a look at a lineup. The three siblings remembered the man who was sitting on the bench. Individually, the kids were asked to pick out the man they saw at the field from the men in the lineup. Each kid picked the same man."

"Was he charged with anything?" Nicole asked with wide eyes.

"He was released. Not enough evidence."

"Was the feeling back then that the man from the field was the same man who attacked Janice Carter?" Claire looked Jack in the eyes.

"The investigators wondered if that was the case," Jack said. "But there wasn't enough to hold the man or charge him with anything so off he went."

"Does he still live around here?" Nicole asked.

"He moved away. I forgot where. Maybe Connecticut? It's in the report."

"From what you know about the case, should we head in a certain direction?" Claire asked. "Is there somewhere you think would be helpful for us to start?"

Jack blew out a long breath. "You could have Gagnon request the autopsy report. Perhaps, the two of you and Detective Gagnon could arrange to visit Janice's former house, just to get a feel for the crime scene."

"Do you think it would be helpful for us to track down the three siblings?" Claire asked. "Talk to them about what happened the night the man tried to abduct the younger sister?"

Jack looked from Claire to Nicole. "Like I said, when time passes, memories can surface that had been suppressed previously. It sure wouldn't hurt to talk to them. Just because other officers have interviewed people and looked at evidence, it doesn't mean you won't find something new when you talk to those same people and consider the evidence. Leave no stone unturned. That will be key."

The young women thanked Jack for his time and for the reports he'd prepared years ago on the case.

Without the report, there wouldn't be much that could be done.

On the way through the house back to the front door, Jack stopped and said, "I just thought of something. After Mr. Adams called the police to report the murder, the first officer on the scene that morning was a young guy. When he arrived, he went inside the house, but he was only a couple of feet inside the door when he stopped. He saw the body, turned, and hurried outside to his cruiser to call for more officers and an ambulance."

A shiver ran down Claire's back as she listened to Jack's remarks.

"I forgot the guy's name, but it's in the report," Jack said. "Track him down. Have him tell you what he saw that day. It will mean more hearing it from someone who was there rather than just reading the report. Ask him questions, jog his memory. Do that with everyone you can find who was involved in the case. That's the way you'll find new information. That's the way you'll solve it."

6

When Claire entered the chocolate shop early the next morning, Nicole rushed out from the backroom with a look of panic on her face.

"I got an email from an event planner. She saw the article in the news when we won the prize at the food festival. She's asking if we'd like to be considered for a big wedding that will be held at an historic mansion about thirty minutes from here."

"That's great." Claire removed her jacket and went to the workroom to hang it up with Nicole following after her. "Why do you look so panicked?"

Nicole said, "We have to prepare the desserts and bring them to the bride's house for a taste test. Others are being invited to take part. It would be a huge contract, a ton of money, lots of promo for the shop."

"That's all good." Claire turned to her friend. "Don't you want to do it?"

"Yes." Nicole looked like she wanted to cry. "But, I got a notice from the building manager. I can't renew my lease here."

"Why not?" Claire's forehead was lined with concern and confusion.

"Someone else approached the manager and offered a lot more money for the space. I have to get out in a month."

"What?" Anger tinged Claire's question. "Doesn't your lease say you have the right of first refusal? Are you sure they can kick you out? Where's the lease? Show it to me." Claire was a corporate lawyer by training and experience, and wanted to read the lease to see if the manager was in his legal right to force Nicole out of the space.

"I have a copy of it in the office safe." In a few minutes, Nicole came out of the shop's office carrying an envelope.

Claire read over the lease while her friend stepped nervously from foot to foot. When Claire looked up, her face was serious.

"It appears there isn't a clause allowing you the

right to first refusal." She folded the papers and stuffed them back in the envelope. "They can kick you out when the lease period is over."

Nicole practically wailed. "What am I going to do? Business is booming. I can barely keep up with it. I don't have time to look for someplace to move. I don't have the money either. I want to accept the offer to prepare bakery items for that wedding, but how can I do it? We're bursting at the seams here."

Claire put her hand on her friend's shoulder. "I think you just pointed out a big problem."

Nicole's teary blue eyes went wide. "What do you mean?"

"Ever since the shop won the grand prize at the food festival, business has exploded. The space here is too small. You need to expand. You need more café space and you need a lot more room for food preparation. If you expand, you can hire more workers, you can add a full-time catering side to the business. You're successful, Nic. It's time to make a business plan spelling out expansion."

Nicole stared at Claire. "I don't know. It will take a lot of money. No bank will give me the line of credit I'll need to do that. I wouldn't be able to afford the loan payments anyway. Expanding will require a ton of money. I can't do it."

A smile spread over Claire's face. "Then I guess it's fortunate that you know someone who can help."

"Who?" Nicole asked before she realized what her friend was saying. "What? You?"

When Claire's husband, Teddy, passed away, he left her his business and more money than she could ever spend in a lifetime. Her financial advisor and several people in her financial services firm knew her net worth and Claire had shared with Nicole that Teddy had left her a good deal of money, but she hadn't revealed the dollar amount. No one else knew that Claire was worth a bundle.

"I can't take money from you." Nicole shook her head vigorously.

Claire tilted her head to the side. "Money is no good unless you share it."

"No. That's crazy. I can't take it from you. That money belongs to you."

"The money actually belonged to Teddy," Claire clarified. "I just ended up with it."

"Oh, I know, but...." Nicole sank onto a stool and put her elbows on the counter so she could hold her head in her hands. "What am I going to do?"

"I think it's pretty simple."

Nicole looked up excitedly. "Wait. What if you

become my partner? You can invest in the chocolate shop if I take you on as an equal partner."

One of Claire's eyebrows shot up.

"We work well together. You have legal and financial experience and you can bake like no one else. Well, besides me." Worry lifted from Nicole's face. "We'll be business partners. You can help me expand. We can share the whole thing."

"But you built this business," Claire said.

"And now I need financial help to expand. Please do it with me."

"I've been thinking," Claire said, "that we should do some cookbooks. The shop has a name now, people in the city know about it, there's been good press since we won the food prize. It might be the right time to do cookbooks."

"I love the idea." Nicole clapped her hands together. "We'll have it all set up legally. Will you do it? Will you join me in owning the business?"

"I'd love to."

Nicole whooped and did a little dance before wrapping her best friend in a hug. "We'll build a chocolate shop empire," she squealed with delight. "It sure was a lucky day when you walked through my door."

"It was a lucky day for me, too." Claire grinned.

"Now we need to contact a Realtor to find us a new place for the shop."

Several knocks were heard at the front door of the store and Nicole groaned. "The shop's not open yet. Why do people think the *closed* sign doesn't apply to them?"

When she went to the front of the store to tell the customer to return later, Nicole called to Claire. "It's Ian."

Claire hurried to greet him as Nicole unlocked the door to let the detective inside.

"I'm beat. I was on a case all night." Ian wrapped Claire in his arms. "I was driving by and decided to stop before heading home to shower."

Nicole brought Ian a coffee and a carrot cake muffin and he sat at the counter to eat while Claire and Nicole prepared the shop for the early morning rush.

"Did you have a chance to read the crime report?" Ian asked.

"We did." Claire filled the cases with bakery items. "There's a lot of good information in the notes."

Ian said, "Jack Phillips wrote a good report, but he didn't include everything that was in the original case file since he never guessed the files would end up destroyed. At least, it's something to go on. Without his notes, the case would be dead in the water. It was a lucky break for us that Jack kept a copy."

Ian went on to explain that he wouldn't be able to spend much time on the case due to too much work in his own department. "If you two will do some of the legwork on the case to help out my detective friend, Keith Gagnon, in Chatham Village, then I'll regularly consult with all of you and give advice." Ian went on, "I'm meeting with Keith for dinner tonight. Can you join us? You can meet each other and discuss the case."

Claire and Nicole agreed.

"The first thing I'd suggest is to talk to the officer who was first at the scene of Janice Carter's murder," Ian said. "Sam Holden. I tracked him down. He's living in Brookline. Shortly after finding Janice's body in the living room of her house, Mr. Holden left the police force deciding the work wasn't for him. He went back to school for engineering. He has his own company." Ian took a small piece of paper from his jacket pocket. "Here's his address. I arranged a meeting for the two of you with him. Keith okayed it."

Claire said, "We read about the attempted

abduction on the young girl near a ball field on the evening Janice was killed. Do you think it's worth finding those siblings and speaking with them?" A nagging sensation had been picking at Claire ever since she'd heard about the man trying to snatch the girl. It seemed too much of a coincidence that both an abduction and a murder occurred on the same night.

"If Keith can find them, I think it would be wise to pay them a visit," Ian said. "Listen to what they have to say. Jack Phillips's notes didn't include a lot about the abduction attempt. I don't believe he interviewed the siblings either. The guy was let off due to lack of evidence so Jack must have thought it wasn't worth pursuing."

Nicole filled three carafes with cream, milk, and fat free milk to set out on the coffee bar. "How likely is it that Claire and I and your detective friend will be able to find anything new on this case?"

"Not very." Ian sipped his coffee and set the mug down. "But if no one tries, then there's absolutely no chance to find the killer."

"You don't think it's a waste of time then?" Nicole asked.

"If there's a chance to bring someone to justice, however slim the chance may be, then no, it isn't a waste of time. And I appreciate that you two will help out." Ian made eye contact with Claire. "You have strong intuition. It's a special skill. An important skill. Not everyone has your ability."

Claire swallowed hard and her heart began to pound.

Did Ian sense her abilities? Did he think she had skills that most people didn't? Was he waiting for her to tell him what she could do?

Her racing heart sank into her stomach.

What if I tell him and I lose him?

7

"When I saw the dead woman on the floor, I knew I would be quitting my job." Fifty-five-year-old Sam Holden sat at the glass table in his engineering and tech office and looked out the window to the Boston skyline. "I nearly passed out when I saw her ... and all the blood." The heavy-set, gray-haired man shook his head as his body gave a shudder. "I can still see it, that crime scene. After so long, after all these years, I can still see the details in the room. The image must be burned into my brain cells."

"It must have been terrible for you." Claire sat opposite the man, watching his face. The misery of walking into the bungalow and seeing Janice Carter dead on the floor was evident in his expression. "You were twenty-five at the time?"

"Yes, I was. A few years younger than the victim," Sam said.

"Can you tell us about the morning?" Claire asked. "What happened when you arrived at Ms. Carter's home?"

Sam blew out a breath. "I was in the squad car driving around the neighborhoods when I got the call. I really didn't think much about it. There was no violent crime in Chatham Village. I thought maybe the woman had fallen and was unconscious or something. I thought the guy who called it in was being overly dramatic."

"You went straight to the house after getting the call?" Nicole asked.

"I did. When I pulled up, the neighbor was waiting. I forget his name."

"Mr. Adams," Nicole reminded the man.

"Right. So I got out of the car and the guy hurried over to me. He looked shook up, kind of pale, he was talking fast. He told me he was raking his front yard when the little girl who lived in the house next door came outside and said her mother was dead. Adams told me he'd peeked into the house and there was a lot of blood in there. I asked if he checked the woman. He said he hadn't. I still figured the woman had simply fallen down and bumped her head."

"What happened next?" Claire leaned forward slightly.

"I reassured the guy and asked him to stay outside while I went in." Some beads of perspiration showed on Sam's forehead. "Then I went inside." A long pause followed his words, and then he shook himself and blinked a few times. "Ms. Carter was on the floor, near the sofa. She had a lot of blood on her. Blood had pooled on the floor. There was a strange smell in the air, kind of metallic. I was told later the smell was from all the blood. I think about that scene and I can still smell it." A look of disgust crossed Sam's face.

"Did you go inside the house?" Claire asked.

"I took a couple of steps inside. I planned to check the woman for a pulse, but I ... I couldn't move my feet. It sounds ridiculous, I know, but my brain froze up. I couldn't make my feet move forward. I started to shake. I got dizzy. I had to get out of there. I whirled around and took off, went back outside." Sam looked down at the tabletop. "I had to gulp in the fresh air. The Adams guy came over to me. He said a few things, but I can't honestly remember any of it. I heard him mumbling, but I couldn't understand a word he said."

"Did other officers arrive?" Claire wished she didn't have to ask Sam any more questions.

"They did. I heard the sirens and it sort of shook me back to life. I was still like a zombie, but I went to my car and called it in. I asked for an ambulance. The dispatcher told me one was already on the way. I knew it wouldn't matter how long it took to arrive. That woman was dead."

"Is there anything else you can tell us about the scene?" Claire hoped Sam could provide more details on what the living room looked like when he stepped into the house.

The man shifted around in his seat seemingly unwilling to dwell on the terrible image. "The sofa was against the wall. The body was on the floor in front of the sofa. On the far wall, there was an open door to a room. I could see an unmade bed in there. A coffee table near the sofa was pushed out of place like it must have been bumped into during a fight."

"Did you see a weapon or anything that could have been used as a weapon?" Nicole questioned.

"I didn't. I could have missed it in my shock, but I think I would have noticed a weapon. Anyway, the officers who arrived and went inside did not find a weapon."

"So the murder weapon was never found?" Claire asked.

"That's correct. It was never found."

"Janice Carter was stabbed to death?" Nicole asked the man.

Sam said, "She was. There were marks on her neck consistent with a strangulation attempt, but according to the medical examiner, the woman died from the stab wounds."

"Did Janice fight back?"

"Yes, she did. There were defensive wounds on her hands and arms."

"We've heard there was no sign of forced entry," Claire said wanting to ask something less upsetting.

"That's right. Ms. Carter must have opened the door to the person."

"Can you describe how Janice was positioned?" Nicole asked.

Sam swallowed again. "She was on her stomach. Her head was turned so her face was looking to the right, to the sofa. Her right arm was out to the side, her hand in a blood pool. Her left arm was under her body."

"Was she clothed?" Nicole asked the question.

"She was fully clothed. A shirt, jeans. Bare feet, though. No socks or shoes." Sam sat up straighter. "I did see a wine glass on the floor."

"Just one glass?"

"I think I heard there were two wine glasses on the floor, but I only noticed the one."

"Two wine glasses," Claire repeated. "If that was the case, then Janice must have known the person. She knew the attacker well enough to serve him or her a drink. What happened?" Claire thought out loud. "Someone comes by, either expected or not. Janice lets the person in, they probably sat on the sofa and sipped the wine. Then what? An argument? An unwanted advance? A kiss or a touch was rebuffed and the person became enraged?" Claire looked at Nicole.

"Did the killer bring a knife into the house?" Nicole asked. "That might indicate premeditation. Or did the killer run to the kitchen, get a knife, and begin his attack?"

Claire asked Sam, "Were these possibilities discussed? Did the detective or the investigators discuss what might have happened in that living room?"

"I avoided the discussion when I could. I gave my notice a week after I was in that house. I worked for two more weeks and that was the end of that. As far as I know, there was never a definitive decision on whether or not the attacker used his own knife or took one from the kitchen."

"What about suspects?" Claire could feel tightness in her temples, an indication that a headache was coming on. "Did the investigators have any suspects in mind?"

"Have you heard about the guy who attempted to attack a little girl? It happened before Ms. Carter was killed."

"We heard someone tried to kidnap a child that evening." Nicole brushed a strand of her dark brown hair from her eyes.

"That's right. The girl and her sister and brother looked at a lineup and the three of them picked out the same guy. The kids said they saw the guy on a bench at the ball field. It had to be him who tried to grab the girl, but he was let go. Not enough evidence against him." Sam put one of his meaty hands on the table. "So the guy goes free. Terrible."

"Do you recall the man's name?" Claire asked. "We heard it was someone named Brandon Willis."

"Yeah, that was him. Willis." Sam said the name like it tasted bad. "If I remember right, the guy only lived in town for about six months. He moved away after being let go. I don't know where he went."

"Had you ever seen Janice Carter in town?" Claire questioned.

Sam's eyes went wide and his breath hitched for a second. "I did see her around town now and then. Sometimes with the little girl. I talked to her once in a pub. A buddy and I went in for a beer. She was there with a friend." Sam shifted his gaze out of the big glass windows. "I thought she was pretty," he said softly. "Huh ... if only there had been some way to have warned her about what was to come." With sad eyes, Sam looked back at the two young women sitting across from him. "I have two sons. I was secretly relieved not to have had a daughter. I would never have been able to let her out of my sight."

Claire's heart clenched at the man's depth of emotion. "Did you know the case files and the collected evidence from the case were destroyed in a small office fire?"

Sam's face took on a look of shock. "I didn't know that. How can the case be re-opened without the evidence? DNA testing was in its infancy back when Ms. Carter was murdered. I thought with the technology today, if you found a suspect, the DNA could be matched to what was collected at the scene."

"It's not to be," Nicole said. "It's all gone. All we have are some notes from a retired detective who looked into the case about ten years ago. The information is far from complete."

"We'll just need to figure out another way to catch the killer," Claire said.

After a few minutes of chat, the young women thanked Sam for his help and stood to go.

Sam walked them to the door and as they were about to exit, he said, "I just thought of something else. Maybe it's in the detective's notes that you have, but that guy who tried to grab the little girl ... he was wearing an unusual hoodie. It was orange. It had something written on it, but I can't remember what it was." The man shrugged. "I don't know why that popped into my head."

A little shiver darted over Claire's skin.

I bet because it's important.

8

The little white lights Claire had strung along the fence at the back of her yard twinkled under the evening sky. Her Adamsburg Square brick townhouse had glass doors off the kitchen that led to a stone patio, a small plot of grass, and a huge shade tree. It was just enough space for the dogs to chase a ball and rest in the grass, and for Claire to grill and have dinner on the patio.

The Corgis lay in the grass and chewed on the ends of a long stick. Ian worked the grill while Nicole and Detective Keith Gagnon stood with him and chatted. Forty-five-year-old Keith was over six feet tall with a muscular build, brown hair, blue eyes, and a warm, friendly smile.

Claire brought out a green salad, a bowl of potato salad, and dish of creamy macaroni and cheese.

"You have a beautiful home," Keith said to Claire as he sipped from his glass of beer. "This backyard is really great."

"I love it here. It helps to have the yard for the dogs."

"And thanks for offering to cook instead of meeting at a restaurant," Keith said.

Ian carried platters with the burgers, kebobs, and veggie burgers to the table and the foursome took seats and dug into the food.

"How did you and Ian meet?" Nicole passed the salad dressing to Keith.

"At a conference," the detective said. "We hit it off right away. We've consulted with one another on a regular basis and we trained together for a few half marathons. I started having some trouble with my hip so no more running for me."

Claire smiled. "Now he makes *me* train with him."

Keith chuckled. "I'm sure Ian prefers your company to mine."

During dessert, the talk turned to the cold case murder of Janice Carter.

Keith said, "I appreciate your help on this case. Ian tells me you're both good interviewers and that you have strong intuitive skills. That's very important. Little things can be overlooked when an investigator misses subtle things in a conversation, body language, facial expression, what the person doesn't say. When you have the ability to pick up on these small details, the little things can lead to a solved case."

"We spoke to the officer who was first on the scene at the bungalow," Claire said.

"Sam Holden." Keith nodded. "It seems the man made the right career choice leaving the police force for engineering. He's very successful."

"Have you spoken with Sam?" Nicole asked.

"I did. About a week ago. He wasn't very forthcoming with me."

"He told us about the crime scene," Claire explained. "He also talked a little about that man, Brandon Willis, who tried to abduct a young girl on the same evening Janice was killed. Police considered Willis a possible suspect in Janice's attack, but the man was let go due to lack of evidence."

"That's right," Keith said.

"Sam also mentioned that Willis was wearing an orange hoodie that night," Claire said. "I suppose the color of the sweatshirt made the man stand out to the kids at the ball field."

"Sam did not share that hoodie information with me," Keith said with a raised eyebrow.

With a smile, Ian set down his dessert fork. "Claire and Nicole seem to have the power of persuasion."

"Then I'm glad you're helping me out." Keith stirred some cream into his coffee. "I don't have a lot of time to devote to this cold case. It was looked into about a decade ago by Jack Phillips and luckily, he took notes. Without those notes, there would be nothing to go on and we'd have to disappoint Janice's daughter, Kelly Cox. Most likely, we'll be giving Ms. Cox disappointing news, but at least, we'll have tried."

"Sam Holden suggested we find the three siblings who were at the ball field the night Janice was killed and talk to them about the orange-hooded Brandon Willis," Claire said. "Their names are in the case notes. The last name was Harrison."

"Did he say why he thought it was a good idea to do that?" Ian asked.

"He didn't say specifically why we should meet with the Harrison siblings," Nicole explained. "I assume to pick their brains about what happened that night."

"I'll do some research and see if I can find out where the siblings are living now," Keith said. "Maybe the three of us can interview them together. I'm going to be away for a few days later in the week and I'll be gone for two days next week. I've told Kelly Cox to contact either of you if she has questions or needs anything. I'll share my contact information with you both. I'll also try to set up a meeting between you and the three Harrison siblings."

"What else should we be doing?" Claire asked.

"I've tracked down one of Janice Carter's friends, Brittany Patterson. She was in nursing school with Janice. I'll email you her address and phone number so you can arrange to speak with her."

"What should we focus on when we meet her?" Claire asked.

"The usual stuff," Keith said. "Ask about their friendship, ask about Janice, what was she like. Ask the woman where she was the night of the murder."

"We're treating the friend as a suspect?" Nicole asked with a look of surprise.

"Everyone's a suspect." Keith drank some of his coffee. "Be suspicious of everyone."

From under the big tree, Bear and Lady let out loud barks of agreement.

∼

"Our lives certainly couldn't have gone in more different directions," Brittany Patterson told Claire and Nicole over coffee at a café in Newton. "Janice was cut down in her prime with so much to live for, her little girl, a future career in nursing. It crushed me. My heart broke." Brittany was sixty-years old, the same age Janice would be had she lived.

"I went on to get my master's degree. I've been a nurse practitioner for years." Brittany had blond hair cut to her shoulders, was about five feet ten inches tall and slim, and gave the impression she worked out or took part in an athletic pursuit of some kind.

"Did you know Janice before you were in nursing school together?" Claire asked.

"We met for the first time in school," Brittany told them.

"What was Janice like?" Nicole questioned.

A wide smile formed over Brittany's mouth. "She was a warm person, friendly, kind, a lot of fun. She was full of life, funny, intelligent. She loved that little girl of hers."

"Did she ever talk about why she hadn't married Kelly's father?" Claire asked.

"She wasn't in love with him and he wasn't in love with her," Brittany said. "I think those are good reasons not to hitch yourself to someone."

"Was Janice dating at the time of her death?" Nicole asked.

"She dated some, nothing serious though. It was hard to get into a serious relationship when there was a little daughter around. Some guys didn't like the idea that there was a child in Janice's life." Brittany smiled as she recalled something her friend had said. "Janice told me if a guy didn't want Kelly around, then she didn't want that guy in her life."

"Did you ever meet Janice's daughter?" Claire asked.

"A few times. I never had kids myself. My first husband and I divorced after a year and my second husband divorced me after two years." Brittany gave a shrug. "Not the marrying type I guess. I focused on my career, my investments. I'm still working full time and I love my job. I'm very good at it."

Claire felt a slight dislike of Brittany and wondered what kind of friend she'd been. The woman answered too quickly, giving vague replies and she took every opportunity to toot her horn about herself and her achievements.

"Can you tell us about the men Janice was dating around the time she was killed?"

"Well, let's see." Brittany rubbed at the side of her face. "I don't recall all of her dates. I do remember she dated a graduate student for a while. I can't recall his name. She went out a few times with another guy, but I don't remember his name either." The woman sat up. "Oh, there was that guy who was accused of attacking a little girl in Chatham Village, at a ball field."

Claire's jaw nearly dropped. "Was his name Brandon Willis?"

"Yes, that's the name," Brittany said.

"You've heard of him?" Nicole's eyes stared into Brittany's.

"I know a few things. I knew he tried to attack the girl at the ball field."

"Are you sure that's the same guy Janice had been dating?" Nicole's voice had risen an octave.

"Yes, it was. I'm sure." Brittany drummed one of her nails on the wood of the table. "Not very good company to keep, was he?"

"Did Janice hope to become more than friends with Brandon Willis?"

"She liked Brandon. He could be funny, he enjoyed being outdoors."

"What happened between them?" Claire considered that one must have broken off with the other.

"I don't really know." Brittany adjusted the scarf she had on. It was bright red with printed geometric patterns of orange and purple. "Brandon was okay. I didn't think he made the best choices. He could seem off socially. I really didn't think those two had any kind of a future together. They were too different."

"How where they different?"

"Brandon liked alcohol. A lot. Brittany might have had a glass of wine once a month, while Brandon was a daily drinker. I warned Janice on numerous occasions about Brandon. The guy didn't work much. He claimed he was self-employed or worked as a mechanic. I never knew what kind of work he did. He always seemed to be hanging around with no purpose."

"Janice didn't listen to your concerns?"

"She did not and our friendship suffered for it for a short time." Brittany looked down at her lap.

"You didn't remain friends?" Claire asked.

"We spoke with each other, but our interactions

lacked the warmth they once did. I learned not to criticize a woman's choice of a man."

"Was that the state of your friendship when Janice was killed? You two weren't as good friends as you were before?"

"It would have blown over." Brittany batted her hand around. "We were on our way back to being good friends, and then ... she was murdered."

The woman's words picked at Claire. Was Brittany's and Janice's friendship close or was it forced? Would Janice have forgiven Brittany for butting into her romantic life and criticizing the man she was dating?

Maybe. Maybe not.

9

Detective Gagnon tracked down Janice Carter's former neighbor and because Gagnon had to leave town for a conference, he asked Claire and Nicole to go and interview the man in Boston. The detective spent a few hours with the young women giving them pointers and suggestions to use when they talked to people about the crime and the three role-played to give them practice with what to look for.

It was early evening, when Claire and Nicole met fifty-seven-year-old Joe Bricklin at a restaurant in the Back Bay. The husky man was bald and Claire couldn't tell if he shaved his head or had lost his hair prematurely. Bricklin had broad shoulders, a small scar on his left cheek, and dark eyes. He was about five feet eleven, looked tough and a little rough around the edges.

"Thanks for meeting with us," Nicole said after shaking hands.

Bricklin gave a shrug and a wry smile. "Didn't really have much choice. When a detective asks you to meet, it's not in your best interest to say no."

They took seats, ordered meals, and got down to business.

"So the Carter case is being re-opened?" Bricklin sipped his beer.

"It's being looked into again," Claire told him. "We're meeting with people who knew Janice or whose paths crossed. You lived across the street?"

"I rented a small house on the street for a couple of years." Bricklin's eyes were intense. "I moved away right after Janice got murdered. I didn't renew the lease. I wanted out of that neighborhood."

"Was there a lot of crime in the neighborhood when you lived there?" Claire asked.

"Absolutely not. It was quiet, the people were solid, no troublemakers or anything like that. Things changed after the killing." Bricklin rubbed his chin.

"You'd met Janice?" Nicole questioned.

"Sure. We weren't friends or anything like that. We didn't get together or do things. We were friendly. When people were outside, they'd talk, ask how things were going. It was a good place to live. You didn't have to worry." Bricklin frowned. "Until you did."

"Do you think the friendly atmosphere and the sense of safety may have contributed to Janice's death?" Claire asked.

"You mean because she wouldn't be afraid to answer the door if someone knocked?"

"That's right."

"If someone knocked or rang the bell, I think Janice would open the door without knowing who was standing there, so yeah, the neighborhood being the way it was did contribute to a creep getting inside."

The meals were delivered to the table and the three ate in silence for a few minutes.

"Do you know anything about Janice's daughter?" Bricklin asked.

Claire set down her sandwich and smiled. "Kelly is doing well. She's a teacher. The case is being looked at again because of her request."

"Good. I'm glad to hear she's doing okay." Bricklin dabbed at his mouth with his napkin. "She asked for the case to be re-opened?"

"She hopes her mother's killer can be found one

day," Nicole said.

"Is it likely? After all these years?"

"It happens," Claire said. "Cold cases can be solved. New information comes to light. People remember things or when time passes, they feel they should come forward and tell what they know."

"Is that's what's happening with Janice's case?" Bricklin asked.

"We hope so." Claire crossed her arms on the table and made eye contact with Bricklin. "We've been told you saw a man at Janice's house on the evening of the murder."

"I was home that night." Bricklin shifted around a little on his chair. "I'd had a couple of beers. I might have been mistaken about seeing someone."

"Oh?" Claire kept her gaze on the man and asked another question. "You thought there might have been a man at Janice's door, but now you aren't sure?"

"I thought I saw someone, but I just don't know."

"What did you *think* you saw that night? What was the man doing?" Nicole asked Bricklin not wanting him to weasel out of what he'd told.

"I was watching television." Bricklin rubbed the top of his bald head. "I got up to go to the kitchen. I thought I saw movement under the streetlight near

Janice's house. I dropped my empty beer bottle and bent to pick it up. When I stood straight, I was looking right out of the window. I thought I saw someone at her door, but now I'm not sure. Maybe it was a shadow."

"What makes you doubt what you thought you saw?" Claire asked.

Bricklin sighed. "I just don't know if I saw someone or not. I don't want to throw the investigation off if I'm not sure about it. It could be a waste of time for the police."

Claire asked, "Did you hear anything that night? The sounds of an argument or a raised voice? A fight? A loud noise? A bottle breaking?"

Bricklin shrugged a shoulder. "I don't think so."

"It was October," Nicole said. "Was it a chilly night or was it warm out?"

Bricklin looked down at his plate. "I don't really remember."

"Was your window open?" Claire questioned.

Again, Bricklin said, "I don't remember."

"How about the next morning? Were you at home when the police arrived at Janice's house?"

"I was at work."

"What did you do for work?" Nicole asked.

"I worked building construction. I was at a house

on the other side of town."

"You left early for work?"

"I left at 7am."

"That was about the time Kelly ran outside to tell Mr. Adams that her mother was dead."

"I didn't see her." Bricklin shook his head, but he kept his eyes on his plate. "I must have left for work before she came out."

"Did everything look normal when you left your house?" Claire asked. "Was anything out of place? Was Janice's front door closed?"

"I'm not sure. I didn't pay any attention."

Claire had the feeling that Joe Bricklin's memory was better than he was admitting. "You didn't see anything that seemed off?"

"No."

"Did you ever date Janice?" Claire looked at the man with a steely gaze.

"We didn't date."

Claire turned to Nicole. "Didn't Detective Gagnon mention that Mr. Bricklin was seen at a pub with Janice?"

Before Nicole could reply, Bricklin said, "A pub? When was that?"

"We could get the information from the detective if that would help you remember," Nicole said.

"Oh, wait. I was at a pub when Janice was there, that's right. It was no date though."

"You interacted with Janice at the pub?"

"We were neighbors. We ran into each other. We talked. It wasn't a date."

"What did you think of her?" Nicole asked.

"She was nice, pretty. She was friendly."

"Did you ever ask her out?"

"I don't think so."

Would you have liked to date her?" Claire asked,

"Sure. I never asked her out though as far as I can remember."

"Were you dating someone else at the time?"

Bricklin pushed back a little from the table. "What's all the interest in my love life?"

"I know the questions make it seem like that's what we're asking about." Claire reassured the man with a smile. "The interest is in who Janice knew, who she hung out with, who her friends were, who she came in contact with. People who knew Janice might be able to point us to someone who could have done her harm. By asking these questions, we're making connections and associations between people."

"I wasn't really dating anyone back then," Bricklin said. "I'd go out with women once in a while, but I didn't find anyone I wanted to be serious with."

"Where did you move to after leaving Chatham Village?" Nicole asked.

"All over. First stop, I went to New Hampshire, then I went on to Colorado for a while. I came back to Massachusetts and got married in Lowell and stayed there for four years. We got divorced and I moved down here, outskirts of Boston, to Somerville, been here about ten years."

"Do you have kids?" Claire asked.

"No kids."

"Did you ever go out with one of Janice's friends?"

Bricklin stared at Claire and blinked a few times. "I went out a couple of times with one of Janice's nursing school friends, Brittany Patterson. We didn't click."

"How did you meet Brittany?"

"She was with Janice at the pub one night."

"Have you kept in touch with anyone from Chatham Village?"

Bricklin said, "Nah. I wasn't close to anyone really. I stayed there two years for work, made a few buddies, but they've moved to other parts of the country."

"Did you ever notice anyone hanging around Janice's place?"

"Outside her place?"

"Outside or going into her place quite a lot."

"Her parents, the little kid. A couple of women would show up there sometimes. That's it, really. I'd see a guy once in a while, but not often."

"Is there anyone you suspected might have been involved with Janice's death?" Claire asked.

Bricklin started to shake his head, but then looked up. "What about that guy who tried to kidnap a girl from the ball field? You heard about that? It happened the night Janice got killed."

"We've heard there was an incident," Nicole told him. "We heard a man was suspected of being the one who tried to grab the little girl, but there wasn't any evidence to take it further so he was released. You think there could be a connection between that person and Janice's killer?"

"It's possible, isn't it? Nothing ever happened in Chatham Village. Then on the same night, a kid almost gets abducted and a woman gets murdered. If you ask me, I'd say the kidnapper and the killer are one and the same."

"Do you know the abductor's name?"

"Brandon Willis," Bricklin said. "He was wearing an orange hoodie when he tried to grab the kid."

"Willis lived one town over from Chatham Village," Claire pointed out. "Did you ever run into him?"

"I ran into him a couple of times at a bar. We played on the same softball team for a while. He sort of gave me the creeps. Something seemed weird about him."

"Really?" Nicole asked. "What about him seemed off?"

Bricklin rubbed at his chin. "I can't really explain it. Just not normal."

"Do you have any relatives, Mr. Bricklin?"

"My ex-wife, if that counts, and my older brother, Mack. He lives about a mile from me in Somerville. My parents are dead. My younger brother died in a motorcycle accident."

"Did you remarry?"

"Nah. What's the point? I don't think I'm the marrying type. I like my privacy. I don't like getting nagged or corrected. I like doing my own thing. I guess I really don't care a whole lot about anyone else."

The words skittered over Claire's skin leaving a feeling of anxiety in their wake.

10

Holding the Corgis' leashes, Claire stood on the busy sidewalk with her face lifted towards the warm sun. Lady, Bear, and Claire waited for Nicole to finish seeing a new space to move her chocolate shop and when she finally emerged from the building, Claire would take a turn looking around inside. Claire had been out for a walk with the dogs when Nicole texted her asking to meet in the North End. A new place had just come on the market and she wanted to be the first to get a look at it.

"There are better places to sunbathe you know, Rollins." A man's voice spoke behind Claire and recognizing the voice, she whirled around to see Bob Cooney.

Cooney, in his mid-fifties, with jet black hair and dark brown eyes had a thin, fit, wiry frame. Wearing black-rimmed sunglasses, slim black dress slacks, a white shirt, and a cashmere camel-hair jacket, the man looked like a very wealthy businessman ... and that's exactly what he was, only the majority of his money had been funded by shady dealings.

Lady and Bear greeted Cooney by dancing around him and wagging their little tails.

"Dog hair," Cooney groaned. "Not on my pants, please." Pretending to be annoyed by the friendly animals, the man's smile and gentle pats on the dogs' heads gave away his true feelings.

"You're looking dapper," Claire said.

"Same to you." Cooney extracted himself from the leashes wrapped around his legs. "Why are you standing on the sidewalk like you got no friends?"

"We're waiting for Nicole." Claire explained that her friend wasn't able to renew her lease and was searching for a new place.

"Why can't she renew?"

"Someone offered more for the space."

"That's unethical for the lessor to do that. Want me to have someone break the landlord's legs?" A former private investigator, Cooney had a reputation for being involved in unscrupulous dealings and making a ton of money from them. He also had a reputation for knowing just about everything that was going on in the city.

Claire rolled her eyes. "No, thank you. I'm sure you'd overcharge for that special service anyway."

"I hear you two are doing some interviews for a detective in Chatham Village." Cooney lit a cigarette and took a long drag, the end of it glowing orange.

"You heard right." Claire let a little bit of leash out so Bear could sniff at spots on the sidewalk. "You shouldn't smoke you know. It's unhealthy."

Cooney took another long drag. "It's my only vice."

Claire snorted.

"Why are you talking to people about a cold case?" Cooney asked.

"Ian asked me to do it. Detective Gagnon is a friend of his."

Cooney eyed the young woman. "Why? Why does that detective of yours need a baker's help? Or is it your legal expertise that he needs?"

"I'm good at understanding people. I have a special skill." Claire wasn't kidding about having a special skill.

"Yeah? What? Are you a witch or something?"

The blood almost drained out of Claire's head.

Cooney asked, "So tell me, has your *special skill* pointed the finger at anyone yet?"

Clearing her throat, Claire said, "Not yet." Narrowing her eyes, she said, "Wait a minute. Do you know who killed Janice Carter?"

Cooney scoffed. "I was just a kid when that woman died."

"You were more like twenty-five," Claire corrected.

"I hadn't advanced in my career yet."

Claire said, "I know that's double-speak meaning you hadn't yet joined up with criminals."

"Always so harsh with me, Rollins." Cooney tsk-tsked. "Don't judge until you've walked in another person's moccasins. I had to do what I had to do. *I* didn't inherit a half-billion dollars."

Claire's eyes flashed. "Neither did I."

"Oh, right. It was more like the full billion."

"I don't know where you get your information." Claire sniffed and changed the subject. "Did you enjoy the chocolate shop sweets I brought you as a thank you?"

"I put on about five pounds eating them. They were delicious."

Claire had brought Cooney a box of bakery items to thank him for giving her a few self-defense tips ... which saved her life not long ago.

"Watch your back on this, Rollins. You go sniffing down a rat hole, you just might smoke one out."

"I'll be careful." Claire smiled. "Since someone recently taught me a few things, I'm pretty good at getting out of a strangle-hold now."

"Don't get cocky. Not with this stuff, anyway. It's dangerous to do so." Cooney rubbed out the cigarette butt with the toe of his expensive brown leather shoe. "I need to get to an appointment. You need any special information to go with your special skill, you know where to find me." Turning away, he bent to pat the dogs. "Tell Nicole *not* to lease this place she's spending so much time looking at."

"Why not?"

"Let's just say, the owner is ... unscrupulous."

"You wouldn't happen to know who the person is who yanked the shop space right out from under Nicole, do you?"

"I do not." Cooney picked a piece of dog hair off of his sleeve.

"Do you happen to know of a better place available to lease?"

The man paused for a few moments. "Take a walk over to Hanover Street." He gave Claire the number. "Inquire in there. Tell the man you're a friend of Bob Cooney. He might be able to help out."

"Thanks."

Cooney started away down the sidewalk. "Watch your back. Tell Nicole to do the same. You want anything, you know where to find me."

Bear and Lady woofed goodbyes to the man.

Cooney's warning made the little hairs on Claire's arms stand up.

~

Claire and Nicole returned to the chocolate shop, made sure the sign was turned to *closed*, and sat at a café table making a list of possible dessert items to present at the taste-test for the wedding job.

"What else did Cooney say about the place we were looking at to move the shop?" Nicole lifted her pen to add another bakery item to the list.

"Nothing else. He said the owner was unscrupulous and not to associate with him."

"Cooney also said the owner of *this* place is dishonest and unethical for kicking me out of here."

"That's right," Claire said.

"It makes me angry. I pay on time. I keep this place in tip-top condition. I treat it like my own place. And the thanks I get is a kick in the pants." Nicole shook her head, a lock of her long brown hair falling out of her loose bun.

"It's better to get out and find something better. Tomorrow we'll have a look at the space the man on Hanover Street has to show us," Claire said. "Do you know what kind of a business is replacing you here?"

Nicole frowned. "A bakery."

Claire groaned. "Well, it won't be as popular as yours, and your customers will follow you to the new place."

"Will they? They're used to stopping here on their way to work or coming in at lunch time. They might not want to change their routine. If it was a market or a clothing store or something different moving in, they might follow me, but with a new bakery here, they might decide not to change their routine."

"Then new people will find you. You are top notch, you have a reputation, you're known now. It will work out. You'll see." Claire made sure her voice sounded confidant and optimistic.

Resting in the corner, Bear and Lady lifted their heads and woofed.

After coming up with a list of ten ideas for the wedding job, the young women decided they'd narrow down the choices over the next few days. Nicole made lattes and she and Claire sat by the window.

"That bald-headed guy we met yesterday rubbed me the wrong way." Nicole sipped the smooth coffee and a bit of the frothy foam covered her lip. "He sure didn't remember much of anything. Did you think he was faking?"

"The thought crossed my mind." Claire looked out at the darkening streets. "I had the distinct impression that Joe Bricklin *did* see something that night ... or maybe, and I'm just speculating out loud ... maybe *he* had something to do with the murder."

"I wondered the same thing," Nicole admitted. "I think he liked Janice. I bet he wanted to date her. Maybe she shot him down. Maybe he watched her go out on other dates from his window across the street and it made him furious."

Claire said, "I was also thinking, what if he did see someone at Janice's door that night? What if the killer found out Bricklin saw him and he threatened Bricklin to make him stay quiet? It would explain why Bricklin changed his story."

Nicole's eyes widened. "That could also be the reason why Bricklin moved away and didn't stay in one place."

Claire nodded. "I felt a little uneasy around Brittany Patterson when we talked with her. Something about her didn't sit right with me, but I can't put my finger on why."

"I agree. She had a falling out with Janice because she criticized a guy she was dating? What in the world did she say about him that would make Janice so angry?"

"Do you think there might be more to the story?" Claire asked.

"We might need to speak with Brittany Patterson again," Nicole said.

Claire's phone buzzed with an incoming text. "It's from Keith Gagnon. He's tracked down the siblings who were involved with the attempted abduction. Sally, Penny, and Bob Harrison. He's set up a meeting for the day after tomorrow so we can talk with them." Claire looked up at Nicole. "Keith also had a meeting with the suspected abductor, Brandon Willis. Keith wants us to speak with him as well. He'd like our input."

Nicole shuddered. "The idea of talking to that guy gives me the creeps."

Claire's stomach tightened with dread.

11

Claire and Nicole met the Harrison siblings in a private room in the Chatham Village library. Sitting at a long glossy, wooden table, thirty-five-year-old Sally Harrison Michaels, had shoulder-length blond hair and big blue eyes. The woman was slim and athletic looking. Her sister, Penny, was forty-two-years old with chin-length light brown hair and the same blue eyes as her sister. She was standing by the window when Claire and Nicole entered the room. Penny was of average height and was slightly overweight. Bob, the middle sibling, was thirty-nine, just under six feet, and had brown hair and a strong build.

After greetings went around the small group, everyone took seats.

"I was pretty surprised to get Detective Gagnon's call," Bob told them. He fiddled with the cuff of his neatly-pressed, pale blue, long-sleeved shirt. "I thought the Janice Carter case was locked up and dead."

Claire said, "Janice's daughter made a request to the Chatham Village Police department to re-open the investigation. We're conducting a few interviews to determine if something new might come up."

"I still think the killer is the same guy who tried to kidnap Sally," Bob said. "I think it's Brandon Willis."

Claire noticed Sally wince at her brother's mention of the attempted abductor.

"Why do you think the same person is responsible for both attacks?" Nicole asked.

"Because some guy tries to grab Sally and a couple of hours later, Janice Carter gets murdered?" Bob shook his head. "Nope. This was Chatham Village. Nothing bad ever happened in this town and then we had two crimes in one night? It has to be the same guy."

Claire looked to Sally who sat with a tight, nervous expression and her hands folded in her lap. "Can you walk us through what happened that evening?"

"Sure." Sally's voice sounded a little hoarse. "It really never gets easier to talk about. We...." She gestured towards her brother and sister. "We were down at the ball field. No one was playing games that evening. It was getting dark. I had my bike and was having a great time riding around the park. Every few minutes, I rode past Penny and Bobby. They were shooting hoops."

"Did you have the park to yourselves?" Nicole asked.

"We did for the most part," Penny said. "Maybe someone walked by now and then, but we didn't pay any attention to them. Mostly the place was empty, quiet. It was fall. It got dark earlier."

Sally said, "We had dinner at home with our parents and then Bobby asked if we could go to the park for a little while. Our mom said to be home before it got dark."

Bobby said, "Penny and I got involved in shooting the baskets, trying to beat each other. We realized we'd stayed out longer than we should have."

"We looked around for Sally, but she wasn't anywhere in sight," Penny said. "We thought she must have biked home. We lived only two blocks from the park."

"So the two of us started walking home," Bob said.

Sally picked up the story. "I biked back to the basketball court. My brother and sister were gone. I got a little scared so I biked fast out of the park." She paused for a few moments, then swallowed hard. "The next thing I knew I was on the ground. I'd fallen from my bike. My leg got scraped. I started to stand up and tried to pick up my bike when someone grabbed my arm. At first, I thought it was Bobby trying to help me up, but then I saw that the person was too big to be my brother."

"What happened next?" Nicole asked gently.

"The bike was in between us. The guy had my arm. I jerked the bike handles and pushed the bike at the guy. I bent my head and bit him."

"You bit him?" Claire was flabbergasted that a little kid would even think to try and bite her attacker.

"Yeah, I did. It was an instinctive reaction. I didn't think about it. I just did it."

"He let you go?"

"He released his grip on my arm and then I took off running and screaming. I think I could hear his footsteps behind me, but he must have veered off when my brother and sister came racing back. They heard my screams."

"I heard a blood-curdling shriek," Bob said. "I'll never forget it. It turned my blood to ice. I knew it was Sally. Penny and I didn't say a word. We both wheeled around at the same time and ran like sprinters back up the street."

"We were lucky we weren't far away. Fate and good fortune were on our side that day." Penny's shoulders seemed to shudder. "If we were any further from the park, I.... I don't think we would have seen our sister again."

"Penny and Bobby raced to me," Sally said. "I was still screaming when they reached me. I could barely get the words out."

Bobby said, "We each grabbed one of her hands and took off for home. All Sally could manage to tell us was that a man was after her. She babbled it over and over. That's all I needed to hear. We were out of there."

"We didn't go back to that park for over a year," Penny said. "And when I did return, I felt sickish. I didn't want to be there. The place scared me. I was suspicious of every man that passed by."

"The incident had a strong impact on the three of us," Bobby admitted.

"I was distrustful of men for a long time. Maybe I still am," Sally said. "I was praised for fighting back. I liked the praise I got for fighting back and being called brave, but I wasn't brave at all. I was frightened nearly to death. I can't even remember the sequence of events. All I recall are the flashes of images, the fall from the bicycle and hitting hard against the pavement, the surprise of it, seeing the person standing next to my bike. I can feel the raw rush of adrenaline and the impulse to fight back. That isn't being brave. That's the will to stay alive."

"It's remarkable, really," Claire said. "You were only five, but you had enough in you to scare off the attacker."

"I think he saw my brother and sister and that's the reason he ran," Sally said. "If Penny and Bobby were slower, well, I bet I'd be dead." Breathing in a long sigh, she told them, "I became a fitness nut. Running, biking, lifting weights. I think subconsciously I have the need to be as strong and fast as I can be, in case I'm attacked again. It's all because of what happened."

Penny looked at her sister with admiration. "My sister is as fit as a person can be. She's run marathons, has completed two Ironman competitions. I'm amazed at her. Me? I stress eat. I eat for comfort. The near-abduction made me feel unsafe in an unstable and dangerous world. I felt there was no one who would be able to keep us safe."

Sally put her arm around her sister's shoulders.

"I'm a chronic worrier," Bob said. "I worry about everything, all the time. I get anxious over nothing. I don't think I'd be like this if Sally hadn't been attacked."

Nicole and Claire uttered some understanding words.

"Did you see anyone lurking around the park that evening?" Claire knew the three of them saw someone there since they were able to pick a man out of a lineup.

"We all did," Bob said. "We didn't think anything of it at the time."

Penny said, "There was a guy hanging around the baseball field, near the basketball courts. He was sitting on a bench. He made some comments to us as we played."

"What sort of comments?" Nicole questioned.

"He made some remarks about our playing, the shots we were making," Bob said. "Minor things like *good play*, *nice basket*. We didn't engage in any kind of conversation with him."

"What did he look like?" Claire said.

"He was probably mid-twenties," Shelly said. "His hair was cut a little longer." She gestured to show Claire and Nicole the length of the man's hair. "It was dark brown. He was tall, skinny."

"He was wearing jeans and an orange hoodie," Penny added.

"Was there anything written on the hoodie?" Claire asked.

"Yes," Sally said with a nod. "Chatham Village Softball. In black letters."

"So he lived in town?"

"For a little while," Bob said. "We found out later that the guy had been in town for only about four weeks. He worked part-time as a mechanic."

"Was he on the town softball team?"

"He joined, but he didn't show up much," Penny said. "The police told us this."

"Had you ever seen this man before?" Nicole asked.

"Never," Penny said. "At least, none of us remember ever seeing him around."

"Was there anything else distinctive about him?"

"No," Bob said.

Penny gave a shrug. "He was drinking a milkshake while he was sitting on the bench. It was one of those big cups with a straw sticking out the top."

"What happened when you got home that night?"

"We raced inside our house," Bob said. "I'm sure our parents were frightened by our report, but they acted calm and confidant. They reassured us, told us we were safe. They called the police."

"When the police showed up, we talked to them individually," Sally said. "They asked a lot of questions. A couple of days later, they asked us to come down to the police station."

"There were men in a line-up," Penny explained. "We were supposed to pick the man who was at the park that evening. We went in one by one. Each of us picked the same man."

"He was arrested?" Claire asked.

"He was brought in for questioning. The police thought they had the perpetrator. Unfortunately, Willis was let off for lack of evidence," Sally said. "I always wonder how many other people he's hurt in his life. Was he going to stop attacking girls and women? I don't think so." Her forehead lined with suppressed anger. "I don't think so at all. But somehow, he keeps getting away with it."

Sally's words made Claire feel ill.

12

"I never touched that little girl," Brandon Willis, the man who allegedly tried to abduct Sally Harrison, said with a hard shake of his head. "Sure, I was at that park. I was just hanging out. That kid says I grabbed her, well, she's lying."

"Why would a five-year-old lie about something like that?" Claire asked.

"Maybe *lying* isn't the correct word to use. That little girl was mistaken. I left the park before those kids did."

Brandon Willis was now fifty-five. His hair was still dark, but the top was thinning. He was no longer skinny, he'd gained some weight and it had settled around his gut like a small basketball. His voice was permanently hoarse from too much smoking.

Detective Gagnon had interviewed Willis before leaving for a conference and told Claire and Nicole that the man was barely able to grunt out a couple of responses to the detective's questions despite being told that the meeting was a formality due to the request from a family member of Janice Carter to re-examine the case.

Detective Gagnon told Willis he wanted to hear the man's account of his experience of being arrested and let go due to lack of evidence regarding the attempted abduction. Willis wasn't having any of it and remained mostly silent during the discussion. Gagnon asked Claire and Nicole to visit the man and see if they could get more out of him.

"Talking to this guy is the last thing I want to do," Nicole said as she piloted the rental car to northern Massachusetts. "Why didn't Gagnon ask another detective or officer to go talk to this man?"

Claire watched the trees zip past. "Because this isn't an open case. Gagnon is doing this research because Kelly Carter Cox asked him to do it. The case is as cold as a winter night. It's thirty years old. No one in his department has time to work on it. Law enforcement doesn't have the resources to direct to this old case. That's why Ian asked if we'd help his friend by gathering information. If we don't find anything soon, Gagnon will put the murder of Janice Carter back on ice."

Nicole groaned. "Fine."

"Brandon Willis was let go. There was no evidence against him. There was nothing to use against him. Nothing at all."

"But the three Harrison siblings claim it was Willis they saw that night," Nicole said.

"People can be mistaken. Willis may have resembled the attacker. The kids saw him in the park and thought he was the one who grabbed Sally. The guy was released by a judge who said there wasn't any evidence against him." Claire wondered why she was trying to convince Nicole that Willis was innocent when she herself was having the same bad feelings about him.

Claire and Nicole sat with Willis in a coffee shop in a small Massachusetts town about thirty minutes north of Boston. Willis's dark hair showed some gray at his temples and he had an overall medium-build.

"Did you notice anyone else around that night?" Claire asked. "Were other people in the park?"

"I know there were some people walking around the paths. It was a quiet night. Not many people were out, but I remember a few were walking the paths and sidewalks."

"What were you doing in the park?" Nicole asked.

"Nothing. I'd been in town. I got a burger and a milkshake. It's only a few blocks from town to the ball field and park so I walked over. I had nothing to do and it was pretty nice out. I sat on the bench and watched the kids shoot hoops."

"Did you see the little girl riding her bike?"

Willis made a face. "I don't know if I actually saw her or I just think I did because there's been so much talk about it. It doesn't stand out to me. Maybe she rode by me and I didn't pay any attention to her."

"You left the park before the kids did?" Nicole asked.

"That's what I said."

"Where did you go?"

"Back to town. I thought I might see a movie."

"Did you hear anyone scream as you walked away?" Claire questioned.

"No, nothing. No screams." Willis rubbed at the stubble on his chin.

"I understand the girl's scream was quite loud," Claire said.

"Well, if she screamed, it didn't reach my ears."

"You were wearing an orange sweatshirt that evening?" Nicole asked.

"That's what they tell me. I didn't keep track of what I wore each day." Willis leaned back in his chair with a sullen expression.

"You owned an orange sweatshirt?"

"Yeah. I joined a softball team. Everybody got the hoodie."

"The Harrison kids told police the person who attacked Sally was wearing an orange sweatshirt," Nicole said.

Willis clasped his hands together and rested them on his stomach. "If that was the brilliant evidence, then the police should have brought in the whole softball team as suspects."

Can you tell us what you did after leaving the ball field?" Claire asked. "Did you end up seeing a movie?"

"I went back to town. The stores were still open, people were walking around. I went over to the movie theatre, but I didn't feel like going inside. The weather was nice and I wanted to stay out so I decided to walk around town. That's what I did. Nothing exciting."

"Where did you go?"

Willis told the young women where he remembered walking.

"That route took you past Janice Carter's house," Claire pointed out.

"I guess it did."

"Did you notice anything when you were out? Did you hear an argument? Angry words? The sounds of a fight?"

"I *could* tell you I heard a woman scream when I walked by Janice Carter's place. That would make you think someone besides me had something to do with her murder." Willis made eye contact with Claire and then Nicole. "But, I won't do that. You know why? Because I'm not a liar. I didn't hear nothing. It was quiet in that end of town. Go ahead, now you can think I killed the woman just because I walked by her house. Just because somebody is in the area where a crime gets committed, it doesn't make that person guilty."

"We're only trying to gather information," Claire explained. "You were released. There was nothing to tie you to any crime. You were in the vicinity of Janice Carter's murder. Perhaps you saw or heard something that didn't seem important at the time, but when looking back, might have significance."

"I don't know nothing." Willis tapped his index finger against his clasped hand.

"You moved out of Chatham Village shortly after Ms. Carter was killed?"

"Yeah. I'm a mechanic. I moved to Chatham Village for a job. It didn't work out. I didn't get along with the owner so I left."

"Where did you move to?"

"Revere for a while, then out to the western part of the state, up to New Hampshire. I like to move around. I get bored easy."

"Then you moved back here to Massachusetts after that?"

"I made a detour to Rhode Island for a while and then to upstate New York. After that, I came here."

"Are you married?"

"Nope. Had plenty of girlfriends though." Willis grinned.

"Are you in a relationship at the moment?" Claire asked.

"I'm single right now." Willis gave Claire a look. "How about you? You free to date?"

"I'm afraid not." Claire straightened.

"How about you?" Willis shifted his gaze to Nicole.

Nicole's upper lip curled slightly in disgust. "I have a boyfriend."

"Well, lucky him." Willis seemed to enjoy making the two young women uncomfortable.

"Had you ever met Janice Carter?" Claire watched the man's face. Janice's friend, Brittany, told them that Janice had gone out with Willis.

Willis crossed a foot over his leg. "I knew who she was. I met her a couple of times."

"How did you meet?" A sensation of unease shot through Claire's body.

"At the softball field."

"Janice played?"

"No, she came with a friend."

"Who was the friend?"

"Some woman. I don't remember her name." Willis leaned his head to one side to get a knot out of his neck muscle.

"What did Janice's friend look like?"

"Blond. Pretty. Looked like a runner. Thin. She was going out with one of the other players."

"Do you remember his name?"

Willis stroked his chin. "Bricklin."

"Janice's friend dated a man named Bricklin? He was on your team?"

"Yeah. I really didn't play much. I got busy with

other things. But I met Janice a couple of times at the field."

"Someone told us that you dated Janice," Claire said.

Willis uncrossed his leg and sat up, a bit of a flush showing on his cheeks. "Who told you that?"

"I don't recall the person's name." Claire had no intention of revealing the identity of the person who shared the information with them.

"I went out with her once or twice."

"That's all?" Nicole asked.

"That's what I said." Willis's tone was angry. "Don't try to link me to the murder because I went out for a beer a couple of times with that woman."

"Are you sure you didn't see Janice more than twice?" Nicole pressed.

"I'm positive." Willis's eyes flashed.

"During the initial investigation, did you tell the police you'd dated Janice?" Claire asked.

"Yes, I did. Didn't you read the case notes?" Willis growled.

"We did." Claire didn't reveal that the case notes had been destroyed and that the information they had from the investigation was limited. She didn't want Willis to discover there might be gaps in what law enforcement knew due to the loss of information. "We want to hear your experiences directly from you."

"Well, I've shared enough about my *experiences*." Willis stood up. "This conversation is over. I don't have to talk to you." The man leaned down, stared into Claire's and Nicole's eyes, and said in a soft, menacing voice, "And don't you dare try to pin that murder on me."

13

In the early morning light, Claire headed along the quiet sidewalks to the North End. It was too soon in the day for the hustle and bustle brought by the people hurrying through the city to their jobs and Claire relished the softness of the morning.

Thinking about the tasks she needed to do once she arrived at the shop, Claire stopped in her tracks. Up ahead, a few doors from the chocolate shop, a couple stood speaking with the building's property manager.

Jim and Jessie Matthews. The owners of JJ's Bakery. The people who co-won the food festival grand prize with Nicole and her chocolate shop pals,

Claire and Robby, and that couple didn't like sharing the prize one bit.

Nicole had run into the couple several times since the festival and each time, Jim and Jessie practically spit in her eye. Their behavior had upset Nicole who was always friendly and helpful to anyone who ran a bakery, café, or restaurant. Nicole lived by the rule that you always give a hand up to someone trying to improve or to make a living as a cook or a baker or a food establishment owner.

A bad feeling ran through Claire and she watched the couple from a distance until they finished speaking with the property manager and disappeared from view. Claire jogged up the street until she had almost caught up with the manager.

"Joel," she called.

The man turned around to see who had spoken his name and his face fell when he saw the blond running towards him. "Oh, Claire." Joel was almost sheepish with her. "Please don't berate me. It's not my fault that Nicole is being kicked out. It's part of my job to present offers to the owner. He is the one who makes those decisions, not me."

"I understand. Are Jim and Jessie Matthews the ones who are taking over the chocolate shop's space?"

Joel looked over his shoulder. "Yeah, it's them."

"Why, though?" Claire stepped closer to the manager. "Did they tell you why they wanted this space so badly that they were willing to pay so much more than the going rate?"

"I don't ask questions like that." Joel shrugged. "If someone makes an offer, I take it to the owner."

Claire's blue eyes darkened. "And he accepts solely on the amount of money offered? Even though kicking out a current lessee who has been a perfect tenant could be considered unethical?"

Joel lifted his hands in a helpless gesture. "It's business, Claire. It's not personal."

Claire looked up the street in the direction Jim and Jessie Matthews had gone. "Oh, I think, in this case, it *is* personal." Making eye contact with the property manager, she added, "And we're going to fight fire with fire. Make an appointment with the building's owner to meet with me." Claire leaned forward and said something in a soft voice to the manager.

Joel's eyes widened. "Will do. How would tomorrow work for you?"

"Tomorrow is perfect."

When Claire entered the chocolate shop after

saying goodbye to Joel, Nicole, in the middle of a rant, was standing at the counter with Robby.

Robby's facial muscles were tight with anger. "Claire. Did you see those two monsters out there?"

Nicole's cheeks were flushed red and her lips were pressed tightly together.

"I assume you mean Jim and Jessie?" Claire headed over to the counter.

"They're the ones moving into my space," Nicole managed to squeeze the words out of her constricted throat as daggers flew from her eyes. "It's their way of trying to run me out of business. Can you imagine anyone being so terrible?"

"There's more than enough business in the North End to support twice the number of bakeries down here," Robby sputtered. "They're just enraged that we co-won the grand prize with them."

"I saw them outside. Those two aren't used to not beating out all the other bakeries." Claire took a drink from a glass of water. "They don't like to share."

"They're arrogant snoots." Robby had his hand on his hip. "They think they can use their money and their clout to put Nicole out of business. She never did anything to them. She's always as nice and helpful as can be. We won that grand prize with Jim and Jessie fair and square."

Claire couldn't help but smile at Robby's forceful defense of his friend and employer.

"Why are you smiling?" Nicole asked.

"There's nothing to smile about," Robby added with indignation.

Claire's eyes sparkled. "Oh, but there is."

∼

CLAIRE AND IAN sat in patio chairs in the backyard of the townhouse sipping from glasses of wine. Bear and Lady had been chasing a ball that Ian threw for them and were now asleep in the grass under the tree. The half-moon was high in the sky surrounded by twinkling stars and the air was just warm enough that a sweater was all that was needed.

Claire had been telling Ian about the interview with Brandon Willis. "I didn't like him. He was kind of arrogant and he was actually threatening at the end of the conversation. I couldn't believe it."

"The guy had a nerve threatening someone who was representing the police department." Ian shook his head in disgust. "I'll let Gagnon know."

"Brandon Willis went out with Janice a couple of times. That surprised me. And Janice's neighbor, Joe Bricklin, was dating Janice's friend, Brittany Patterson. I feel like I need a chart showing the relationships and connections between people. Joe Bricklin never mentioned he was dating Janice's friend. Why wouldn't he tell us that?"

"Most likely, he wanted to distance himself from Janice thinking it would prevent him from being considered as a suspect."

"Lying about his connections make me suspect him more." Claire took a sip of her wine. "Does he have something to hide?"

"When Gagnon gets back from the conference, it might be a good idea for him to talk to Bricklin." Ian reached for Claire's hand. "You really have a gift for picking up things from people. You're a natural investigator."

Keeping her *talent* from Ian made Claire feel like a liar. She glanced over at Lady and the dog looked her in the eye and woofed.

Sucking in a long deep breath, Claire made the decision. Setting her glass down, she faced her boyfriend. "I've been waiting for the right time to tell you this."

Ian faced her, his dark brown eyes questioning. "What is it?"

"It's hard to talk about ... because I don't quite understand it myself."

Ian's head tilted to the side. "You can tell me, Claire."

"Can I?" Claire lifted her eyes to Ian's. "Will you promise that what I tell you won't make you change your mind about me?"

A little smile crept across Ian's lips and when he saw that Claire wasn't kidding with him, the smile dropped away and he said, "You're serious."

"I'm dead serious."

Ian searched Claire's face. "Nothing you tell me will change how I feel." The man took both her hands in his and held tight. "I love you, Claire."

Tears filled her eyes and she brushed them away and cleared her throat. "You haven't heard anything like this before," she warned.

Ian's smile returned. "I've heard a lot of stuff."

Claire repeated, "You've never heard anything like this before."

"Then you'd better tell me so I can add it to the list of crazy things I've heard. The suspense is killing me."

"I have more than one thing to tell you."

"So much the better."

Feeling sick with worry, Claire bit her lip and then began her tales starting with her growing up years in near poverty with a loving and devoted mother, her education and experience as a lawyer, and her two-year marriage to a man forty years older than herself.

"You're amazing, do you know that?" Ian told her. "Your intelligence, your perseverance, your hard work, your belief in doing the thing that matters to you despite naysayers and convention. Teddy was lucky to have you, and so am I."

When a glistening tear slipped from Claire's eye and slid down her cheek, Ian reached over and wiped it away.

"I have one more thing to tell you," Claire said.

Bear and Lady stood up, crossed the grass, and took positions on either side of their owner.

"I'm ready," Ian told her.

"I have ... um ... I have sort of a special skill."

"You have more than one," Ian smiled.

"This is different." Claire watched Ian's face. "Tessa calls it a paranormal ability."

Ian's eyes widened as one eyebrow went up.

"But I think of it as a heightened ability to

sense things, to feel things about people or situations, to pick up on things going on around me." Claire paused for a moment. "I think everyone could probably do it, but for some reason it gets buried inside others and can't come out, while I ... I...."

"You shine," Ian said softly. "There's something extra in you. I'm not surprised that you're able to pick up on things the way you do. It makes so much sense."

Bear and Lady jumped up and danced around Ian's chair causing him to laugh out loud. Lady licked his hand before Ian scratched both dogs behind their ears. "I think they approve of my reaction."

"We've been afraid to tell you." Claire grinned at the sweet Corgis, and then she told Ian how the strength of her ability increased after losing Teddy and moving to Boston. She gave him details and examples of things she'd been able to perceive and figure out by using her skills.

"Sometimes, the messages aren't clear at all and I struggle. This cold case is like that. It feels like the threads of information are all tied up in a huge knot. Other times, I feel things clearly as if the things I need to know are being whispered in my ear."

Ian asked a million questions and Claire answered as best she could.

"Does it bother you," she asked Ian, "this unusual thing I have that I can't really explain?"

"Not one bit." Ian smiled broadly. "Can you teach me how to do it?"

14

When the doorbell rang, Claire and Ian startled and the dogs barked. They went to the door and were surprised for a second time to see Janice's daughter, Kelly Carter Cox, standing on the top step.

"Do you have a few minutes?" Kelly asked. "I'd like to talk to you."

"Kelly, come in." Claire, Ian, and the dogs led the young woman out to the patio.

"It's so pretty out here," Kelly said, as she took a seat in one of the chairs.

"How did you know where I lived?"

Kelly looked a little surprised by the question. "I did an internet search."

"Have you talked to Detective Gagnon recently?" Ian asked.

"He's at a conference and I wanted to show someone what I found." Kelly shifted her eyes from Claire to Ian. "Is it okay? Should I wait for Detective Gagnon?"

"I don't think there's any reason to wait," Ian said. "You can get in touch with Gagnon when he gets back."

"Okay." Kelly relaxed and reached into the bag to remove a manila envelope. "I've been thinking about my mother's death. I've been reading everything I can get my hands on about the case. Some things I'm not sure if I actually remember or it's just that I remember people taking about it."

"You found something?" Claire's heart was pounding.

"My grandfather loved to take photographs." Kelly pulled some pictures from the envelope. "He photographed everything. This is the house we lived in." She placed a photo on the patio table. "This is the house where my mother died." For several seconds, Kelly's eyes were pinned to the photo until she blinked fast a few times and took a deep breath. "I forgot I had these. I only remembered today that I had them. Have you been to the house?"

Claire and Ian both shook their heads.

"I don't know if these will be of any help, but I wanted to show them to you." Kelly placed a second photo on the table. "This is me standing on the front steps of the house. It was taken a couple of days after my mom died."

Claire stared at the picture and her heart clenched.

"I don't know why my granddad took these interior shots. Maybe for insurance purposes? It seems odd to me that he shot these photos." Kelly placed three pictures on the table facing Claire and Ian. "This is the living room. This is where my mother died."

A chill raced over Claire's skin and she had to keep herself from gasping.

The photo in the middle showed the sofa, a coffee table askew, the door to Kelly's bedroom, and blood. Lots of blood. The body had been taken away, but the blood on the floor next to the sofa almost created an outline of where Janice's body had fallen. Blood spray and spatter where evident and large pools of blood had gathered in two spots.

"The crime scene," Claire whispered.

"Is it any help to see these photographs?" Kelly

asked. "Have you found any photos the police took back then?"

"We haven't seen any photos at all," Ian told her as he leaned closer to the pictures.

"There's a large pool of blood on the sofa," Claire pointed out. "Janice must have been attacked while she was sitting on the sofa."

"And then she fell to the floor either from fighting the attacker or from losing consciousness," Ian said.

Something about the picture made Claire want to recoil, but at the same time, there was something about it that drew her to it. She lifted the photo and brought it close to her eyes. "There's something here on the floor."

"Where?" Ian squinted.

"See here? It almost looks like a letter." Claire pointed without touching the picture.

Ian swallowed. "Written in the blood?"

"Can this be enhanced?" Claire questioned.

Ian asked Claire to scan the photo to her laptop and when that was done, he brought up a photo editing software package Claire had installed. Clicking away to manipulate the image in the photograph, Ian was able to enlarge and zero in on the spot Claire had pointed to.

"Right here." Ian's voice was excited. "Look at that."

Claire was speechless. The photo showed the letters, BR, written in blood on the floor.

Ian looked up at Kelly. "Your mother had to have been alive when she hit the floor. She used her finger to write us a message ... a partial message anyway."

"BR," Claire repeated.

Kelly said, "That's what I thought I saw, the initials, BR."

"Brandon?" Claire asked. "Brandon Willis, the guy who was questioned about abducting Sally Harrison when she was five-years-old."

"How about Bricklin?" Ian asked. "The neighbor, Joe Bricklin."

"BR," Claire muttered. "If only Janice could have managed to write a couple of more letters."

"Does it help? The letters?" Kelly asked.

"It's great information," Ian praised Janice's daughter. "Would you mind if I take this photo to the crime lab for technical enhancement?"

"You can gold-plate it if it helps find my mother's killer," Kelly's tone was serious.

"I'll alert Detective Gagnon about the photo," Ian told the woman.

"Do you think it will it help find the killer?" Kelly's voice was like that of a child.

"I think it could," Claire reassured her. "If the enhancement works, we might be able to see more."

"Sometimes we lose clarity and quality when a picture is enhanced or enlarged," Ian explained. "Let's hope the enhancement won't degrade the quality of the photo."

The three of them looked through the other crime photos Kelly's grandfather had taken of the house where Janice was murdered. The kitchen, a view of the living room taken from Kelly's bedroom door, the hallway that led to Janice's bedroom. None of the other pictures had the impact of the first one. Those markings written in blood ... were they a message from Janice? Was she trying to name her attacker?

Claire looked up. "Since you've been focusing on the murder, have you recalled hearing anything that night? Angry words? The sounds of a scuffle?"

Kelly shook her head. "It's like I wasn't in the house that night. How could I have slept through someone attacking my mother? Did she not cry out? Was she afraid to wake me? Was she afraid if I got up, then the killer would have hurt me, too? There had to be noise. How did I not wake up?"

"Kids can sleep through anything," Ian told her. "It's not unusual."

"If you did wake up, you may have been so frightened by what you heard that you hid under the blanket and ended up falling back to sleep," Claire speculated.

Kelly sighed. "I just don't know. My poor mother. Will the case ever be solved?"

"I promise we'll do everything we can," Claire assured her. "You mentioned Brittany Patterson being a friend of your mother. Do you remember her?"

"A little. She came to the house sometimes," Kelly said.

"Did you like her?"

Kelly's nose turned up a little. "Not so much. She didn't seem to like kids."

"Why do you say that?" Claire asked.

"Just a feeling I got. It seemed like she wanted me to go away, go in my room when she was visiting. She'd say hi to me and act sweet, but it seemed fake. I was only five, but I didn't like the way she treated me."

"What about the other neighbor?" Claire asked. "The man who lived across the street. Joe Bricklin. Do you remember him?"

"A little. He used to come over to talk to my mother whenever we were out in the front yard."

"He was a friendly man?"

"He was to my mother. He ignored me."

"Was your mother friendly to him?" Claire questioned.

"Not overly so," Kelly said. "She seemed … polite. She really liked Mr. and Mrs. Adams, the couple who lived next to us. They were so nice. Once in a while, she invited them over for tea."

"Did she ever invite Joe Bricklin inside?"

"Never. At least not that I know of."

"Did your mother ever have a man over for dinner or drinks?"

Kelly's forehead creased in thought. "Once in a while. Not often, as far as I can remember. Sometimes she went out and my grandmother would babysit me. Grandma was fun. We'd play games, she'd read to me, we'd watch a show together." Kelly sighed. "She changed after my mother died. She was always so sad. I didn't understand it back then. I didn't connect her sadness to losing her only child. That killer didn't just take my mother's life, he ruined my grandparents' lives, too. He stole from me and my grandparents. He ripped our hearts right out of our chests."

Claire looked across the table at Ian and saw her own emotions, sorrow for Janice and her family and resolve to find the killer, mirrored in his eyes.

15

Claire and Nicole met Janice Carter's friend, Lisa Wall, at a restaurant in Boston. Sixty-year-old Lisa was of medium height, fit-looking, with short blond hair and friendly, blue eyes.

"I'd known Janice since middle school. When Janice was killed, my husband and I lived two towns over from Chatham Village. I worked in Boston as an immigration attorney. I sold my practice a few years ago. Now I teach law at one of the universities."

"Did you keep in touch with Janice back then? Were you still friendly with her at the time of her death?"

Lisa's blue eyes seemed to cloud over. "I sure was.

Janice was like the sister I never had. We were two peas in a pod. She had her daughter when she was twenty-five. Janice worked as a dental hygienist, but she wanted to be a nurse practitioner. I encouraged her to go back to school and do it."

Nicole said, "We heard she was working and going to school. It couldn't have been easy to do all of that with a little child to take care of."

"Janice wanted to make something of herself," Lisa said. "She wanted to be a good role model for her daughter. She worked darned hard." The woman paused for a moment. "So many years have passed ... and I still miss her."

Claire nodded. "We're trying to put the pieces together. Janice's daughter, Kelly, asked that the case be re-opened. Evidence and the case notes were destroyed in a minor fire so all we have to go on is a report that summarized investigative research from the case. The details are missing. We're working with the police to interview people who knew Janice."

"With the case notes and evidence gone, it will be an uphill battle to find anything helpful after so many years," Lisa said.

"We're giving it a try," Claire told her. "For Janice's daughter."

"How can I help?" Lisa lifted her coffee mug to her lips.

"You saw Janice regularly back then?"

"We'd get together two or three times a month. Most of the time, I went to her house. That way, Kelly didn't have to have a babysitter and Janice could be home to put her to bed. Kelly was a sweet kid. The three of us would eat dinner and then we'd play games or read together."

Claire liked the way Lisa talked about Kelly and how she'd interacted so nicely with the little girl so many years ago. "Can you tell us how Janice was feeling around the time of the attack? Was she worried about anything? Did she talk about anyone bothering her?"

"Janice was pretty. She was friendly. People were drawn to her. She always had some guy barking up her tree, trying to date her, wanting to go out with her." Lisa's face became serious. "Some guys wouldn't take no for an answer. They'd keep calling her. They'd show up at the door. They'd send her flowers. It sounds great, right? It wasn't. It was a real bother. Janice was a busy person ... she had a child, a day job, attended school at night. Occasionally, she enjoyed dinner or a drink with a guy. She always told them she couldn't enter into a serious relationship at that point in her life."

"Some didn't listen?" Claire asked as a skitter of worry slipped over her skin.

"That's right," Lisa said. "They'd bother her until she wouldn't answer their calls anymore. She would become angry at their unceasing pestering. She decided it was too much trouble to go out with male friends anymore so she stopped accepting invitations."

"Had she gone on any dates around the time of the murder?" Claire asked.

"She'd been invited out, but she declined."

"Do you know if someone was interested in her back then?"

"She'd gone for a drink with that guy who was questioned about the attempted abduction. You've heard about that? His name is Brandon Willis. I think they went out a couple of times."

Claire and Nicole nodded.

"We spoke with him," Claire said.

"Well, Brandon wanted to go out again, but Janice got the impression he was looking for a serious relationship so she told him she couldn't meet up again." Lisa frowned and shook her head in disgust. "Brandon started stalking Janice. He'd show up places and just stare at her. It was unnerving. I was with her once when he showed up. He was so weird. Jeez. There are plenty of other women in the world. Go find one who is interested in dating you. Did he actually think he could win her over by appearing out of nowhere and gawking at her?"

"Did it eventually stop?" Nicole asked.

"Only because Janice died." Lisa ran a finger over the handle of the mug.

"Brandon Willis was still bothering Janice then?" Claire asked.

"He was."

"Do you think he had something to do with Janice's death?"

"I can't say one way or the other," Lisa's eyes were sad. "I'd love to say it was Brandon, but how do I know? I can't point the finger at him just because he was odd."

"We heard that just before Janice was killed, she and her friend, Brittany Patterson, had a falling out," Nicole said. "Do you know anything about that?"

Lisa sighed. "Brittany was always a drama queen. I didn't care for her. She came off like she was your best friend, but then she'd say something mean or she'd ignore you. I told Janice that Brittany was just a user. She wanted an audience, someone she could brag to. Janice was too nice. She could see how Brittany was, but she felt bad pulling away from her and always ended up being friendly again."

"We heard that Brittany dated Janice's neighbor, Joe Bricklin, for a while," Nicole mentioned.

"I met Joe. I didn't like him either. He seemed to pay too much attention to Janice even though he was dating Brittany."

"How do you mean?"

"I was over at Janice's a few times," Lisa said. "We were out on the front lawn playing with Kelly. Joe would dart over as soon as he saw us and would smile at and chat with Janice. He beamed at her so much I thought his teeth would fall out of his mouth. Janice told me she thought he was a little too friendly. I agreed. We stayed in the backyard after that."

"Joe claimed he saw someone at Janice's door that night," Claire said.

Lisa's steely eyes looked from Claire to Nicole. "Oh, really? That's convenient, isn't it? Did he say that to take attention off of himself?"

"You think he should be a suspect?"

"Why not? An unrequited crush. Living across the street, seeing Janice every day. If you saw the way he looked at Janice, you'd slap his name right at the top of the list."

As Claire thought back over the interviews she'd done on the case, a million feelings of unease pummeled her. Did people lie to her? Did people deliberately place suspicion on others to take attention from themselves? Joe Bricklin claimed to see someone at Janice's door, but then said he was probably mistaken. Brandon Willis told Claire he only dated Janice once or twice because they weren't a good match, but Lisa claims Brandon was obsessed with Janice. Brittany reported that she and Janice had a close friendship despite a minor falling out over a comment she made about Janice dating Brandon Willis. Lisa claimed that Brittany was a user and Janice was only friendly with the woman because she would feel badly about ending the friendship.

Bits of conversation floated on the air and swirled around Claire making her dizzy and unable to grasp at the truth. She made eye contact with Nicole and her friend picked up on her distress and took up the conversation to give Claire time to calm herself.

"How did you find out Janice had died?" Nicole asked.

Lisa took a deep breath. "Janice's mom called me. It was devastating. It was heartbreaking. Mrs. Carter was sobbing into the phone. When I heard her, I knew Janice was gone. I didn't have to hear the words. I barely heard what she said to me. My head was buzzing. I'll never forget it." Lisa wrung her hands together. "My next thought was of Kelly. Was she okay? I got in the car and drove to Chatham Village as fast as I could. When I got there, I hugged Kelly. I was so thankful that little girl was fine. I was going to invite her to stay with me and my husband, but it seemed best that she should stay with her grandparents so they could be a comfort to one another."

"Did you keep in touch with Kelly?" Nicole questioned.

"I saw her a couple of times a month until she moved away to live with her aunt. I sent cards and then emails. I went to her graduation from college." Lisa let out a long breath of air. "Janice would be so proud of her."

"Can you think of anyone else we should talk to?" Nicole asked.

Lisa shrugged. "I don't know. You've probably talked to everyone I can think of. Why can't the killer be found? Why does it have to be so hard?"

"If the initials 'BR' were found at the scene," Claire asked, "who would first come to mind as the killer?"

Without hesitation, Lisa said, "Bricklin. Joe Bricklin."

16

When Ian placed the enlarged and enhanced crime scene photo on her kitchen counter, Claire had to suck in a breath and close her eyes for a second.

"Looking at these kinds of photos never gets easier," Claire whispered.

Ian said, "I've been in law enforcement for thirteen years and I always wince when I have to look at crime scene photographs. If I ever become hardened to such things, well, that will be the time I should leave the job."

Claire's eyes slowly moved over the picture of Janice Carter's body face down on her living room floor, her arm outstretched, her finger resting next to the letters she so bravely wrote in her own blood.

Focusing on the red letters on the floor, Claire tried to block out the rest of the image. BR.

Janice most definitely knew her killer and she attempted to write out her attacker's name so the police would know who was responsible for her death.

Claire's vision began to dim and she clutched at the countertop to steady herself, when Ian noticed and took hold of her arm.

"Are you okay?"

"I feel a little dizzy." Claire raised a hand to her temple.

"Come, sit down." Ian led her to a dining room chair. "It's very upsetting to see the photograph."

"I need to see it. Would you bring it over here to the table?" A chill had rushed over Claire's skin making her shiver and when Ian carried the photo to her, she forced herself to look.

The upper-case letters seemed to lift off the floor and hover a few inches in the air. They shimmered and changed their form to lower-case, and then altered from block letters to cursive.

Claire blinked a few times, but kept her gaze pinned on the BR.

The letters changed back to lower case and slowly fell back to the floor, but just before they touched down, what seemed to be a third letter began to show next to the BR.

Claire leaned closer and squinted, but just as she thought she could make it out, it disappeared.

She let out a long sigh and Ian asked her what was wrong. When she told him about a third letter beginning to form, Ian's face took on a skeptical expression, but it vanished right away when he recalled his girlfriend's special skill.

"Do you think there's another letter? Did Janice write a third letter?" Ian bent to look closer at the photo.

"I don't think it's visible," Claire said. "I think it can only be seen in my mind."

Ian straightened in his seat. "Oh. I see. Could you make out what letter it was?"

"I didn't have time. It sank back into the blood." Claire squeezed the bridge of her nose.

"Is this skill of yours ... a burden?"

"Sometimes." Claire gave a slight nod. "Tessa says this isn't unusual, that the skill will swing from strong to weak. She said it will probably become easier to control as it becomes better developed and I get more used to it. For now, it's unpredictable and can desert me when I need it most. It's very frustrating."

Ian made tea and he and Claire and the Corgis retreated to the living room to relax.

"You need to rest." Ian handed Claire a mug. "This thing of yours ... it's probably best not to try and force it. It's most likely the kind of thing that needs to blossom on its own and can't be forced. Take a break from it. Don't look at the photo again for a couple of days."

A little smile played over Claire's face. "You know a lot about paranormal stuff, huh?"

"No, but I have a lot of common sense." Ian grinned as he placed an arm around Claire's shoulders.

"Probably one of the most important of all characteristics," Claire told him.

Deciding to take a rest from the case, Claire and Ian watched a movie sitting in the middle of the sofa with the dogs like a pair of bookends, one Corgi to the left of Ian and the other one pressed against Claire's right side.

Snuggled next to Ian and a warm, furry dog, Claire couldn't recall a time when she'd felt so relaxed, comfortable, and safe.

CLAIRE TOLD her friend about the experience of seeing another letter in the blood as she and Nicole strolled around the periphery of the Boston Common while the Corgis ran and played with the other dogs on the hill.

"It was startling. It came out of nowhere. All of a sudden, a letter seemed to be emerging, but then it was gone before I could make out what it was."

"Like Ian said, don't push," Nicole told her. "Take another look in a couple days and see if it happens again. Ian really took the news about this thing of yours in stride."

"Thankfully. It was a huge relief. He doesn't look at me like I'm a nut or a kook or a whack-o. He accepted the whole thing with ease. It's pretty amazing that my best friend and my boyfriend accepted my skill so matter-of-factly. I don't know how I found you two."

Nicole said, "Robby knows you have some kind of ability, too. He's very perceptive. You can't hide anything from him."

Claire raised an eyebrow and chuckled. "Maybe Robby will one day show signs of having a skill of his own."

"Oh, gee." Nicole shook her head. "I'm not sure I

can handle two paranormal wizards in the store with me."

Claire's phone buzzed and she lifted it to her ear to take the call from Detective Gagnon. After listening for a minute, she said, "Right now? But Nicole and I are on the Common. We have my dogs with us." Claire's face took on a look of surprise. "Okay, if you're sure."

When she slipped the phone into her pocket, she told her friend, "Detective Gagnon has arranged with the owner of Janice Carter's former house for us to visit it. Now. He said to bring the dogs. He's on his way here to pick us up."

Gagnon's car pulled into the short driveway of a pretty, rustic bungalow on a street of similar homes in a quiet neighborhood. Window boxes spilled over with flowers, a picket fence edged around the yard, and there was a small, welcoming front porch.

The three people and the two dogs stood next to Gagnon's car looking at the place.

"Hard to believe someone was murdered in this house," Nicole said. "It looks so homey and nice."

A prickly feeling bounced over Claire's skin. Despite the well-tended, inviting look of the house, she could feel the horror of the past brushing up against her.

Lady whined and Bear made a low rumbling sound in his throat.

"The woman who owns the place is out for a few hours," Detective Gagnon told them. "She said she was glad to have us look around if it might help solve the crime. She left the door unlocked."

"How does she live here without having nightmares all the time?" Nicole asked. "I don't think I could live in a murder house."

Claire's throat tightened at Nicole's words and she shivered. A murder house.

"Shall we?" Gagnon led the way inside. "As you know, there was no sign of forced entry. Janice must have opened the door to the person. She must have known the killer since she started to write his name in the blood."

Bear and Lady entered the house with their nose to the floor.

Claire leaned close to Nicole and whispered, "Catch me if I pass out."

Nicole gave her friend a look of a concern.

"We have the owner's permission to look around in the rooms. That door over there on the other side of the living room goes to the child's bedroom."

A sofa was placed against the wall with a coffee

table in front of it in the same configuration that Janice's furniture had been.

"There was blood on Janice's sofa here." Gagnon pointed to the new owner's couch. "There was quite a lot of it which makes it appear that the attack started on the sofa. The attacker must have inflicted a number of stab wounds while Janice sat there."

"Would that indicate a sudden burst of anger?" Nicole asked. "Janice and the person must have been talking together if she was sitting on the sofa."

"That's possible," Gagnon said. "Janice and the attacker could have been conversing as they sat together. For whatever reason, the killer became enraged and began to stab Janice. Another scenario is that the killer ordered Janice to sit down and then began his attack on her."

Claire began to feel ill. The edges of her vision began to darken and fade.

"Janice must have fought back," the detective said. "The coffee table was askew so they must have fought right here. We assume the knife attack continued and eventually Janice fell to the floor. The killer took off thinking Janice was dead, but she was still alive. She had time to mark out the two letters before succumbing to her wounds."

Claire's ears buzzed. She could feel the chaos in

the room. The desperation of a young mother clinging hard to life so her child would not grow up without her. Claire saw the glint of the blade and choked on the attacker's fury.

Janice did not cry out. She couldn't risk waking up her daughter, she had to keep Kelly safe.

The young woman fell to the floor. The killer ran out the door.

Janice turned her head and rested her cheek against the glossy wood floor. Her hand moved. Her finger haltingly traced a letter, then a second one.

Make the third letter, Claire urged.

The finger touched the blood.

Thump-thump ... thump-thump ... thump....

Silence.

Janice's heart stopped beating.

17

Tony handed Claire the last can of soup from the carton so she could place it on the shelf. Unable to sleep last night, she was up early so she and the dogs headed down to Tony's market. Even Augustus hadn't arrived yet for his morning coffee and newspaper.

"I'm glad you dragged yourself down here early today," Tony said. "I wouldn't have been able to stock the shelves so fast without you." He wiped his hands on his apron.

Claire had been telling Tony about the case she and Nicole were helping with. "I didn't like being in Janice Carter's former bungalow. The idea of her getting killed in that house really made me feel awful. My head was spinning. I thought I might pass out."

"Well, if you did faint, Nicole and the detective were there to catch you." Tony broke down the cardboard box with his meaty hands. "No shame in feeling someone else's pain and loss. It's not a sign of weakness to be sensitive to such things, it's a sign of strength."

"I sure didn't feel very strong when I was in that house yesterday."

Lady walked down the store's skinny aisle and paused to give Claire a lick on the hand.

"Good dog." Claire patted the Corgi on the head.

"Did being in the house help with any clues?" Tony asked.

"Not really." Claire pushed her blond curls into a high ponytail and started to count the day's money into the cash register. "It was more just to get a feel for the space. The little daughter's bedroom is right off the living room. The fight in the living room didn't wake the daughter. The attack must have been over pretty fast. It seems clear that Janice must not have screamed to prevent her daughter from waking up and coming out to see what was happening."

"That was a brave woman," Tony said. "The daughter had to be her number one priority."

Claire brought up the letters written on the floor. "Imagine having the presence of mind to try and write out the killer's name."

Tony paused in preparing the deli meats and cheeses and looked across the room at nothing. With a sigh, he said, "I can't imagine it. I hope Detective Gagnon can piece together what you, Nicole, and he know so the monster will be arrested."

Claire was about to say something when Tony waved his hand. "Oh, I know it will be next to impossible to make an arrest, but miracles happen, Blondie. Don't give up on it."

With a smile, Claire told the man, "I was about to say, I'm not going to give up on Janice. I'll do whatever I can to find the man who stole her life from her and who stole a mother away from her daughter."

"I knew you'd do nothing less." Tony gave her a nod. "So, as it stands, who are you leaning towards as the killer?"

"That's the problem," Claire said. "No one stands out. A case can't be made against anyone yet. That's why Brandon Willis wasn't arrested and brought to trial thirty years ago. Even though suspicion can be cast on a few people, there isn't a shred of evidence to charge anyone."

"Does your intuition point to anyone?" Tony placed a stack of paper bags under the counter.

Claire gave the man a look. Tony didn't know about her special skill, but when he mentioned her intuition, Claire's heart skipped a beat. "There's Joe Bricklin, the neighbor. Years ago, he claimed to have seen a man at Janice's door that night, but he's retracted the statement saying he isn't sure any longer. What he saw might only have been a shadow."

"You think he might have made up seeing someone there? Maybe he wanted to be part of the excitement swirling around the investigation, so he made up a story about seeing a person at the woman's door," Tony said.

"I wondered about that," Claire said. "I think it's possible that over the years, Bricklin might have regretted giving the police false information. I also think it's possible he could be a suspect."

"What about the child abductor? Brandon Willis?"

"In my mind, he's a suspect. I don't care if he was let go due to lack of evidence. The Harrison kids picked him out of a line-up. He dated Janice a couple of times. He didn't like getting dropped by her. Brandon was sort of stalking her. He could have been hyped up and seething that night, maybe he'd taken some drugs. He lashed out at a little girl and knocked her from her bike, then he ran away. Brandon Willis could easily have ended up at Janice's house looking for revenge because she stopped dating him."

"That's a frightening thought." Tony's facial muscles looked tight. "Well, actually any scenario you could come up with is frightening."

The market's door opened and Judge Augustus Gunther entered the shop dressed in a blue, well-tailored suit, a meticulously pressed white shirt, and a blue and yellow tie. "Good morning. Am I later than usual? Have I missed an interesting discussion?"

Claire brought the former judge up to speed on where the case stood and told him about visiting the house where Janice Carter lived when she was murdered.

"Do you think the murder was premeditated?" Tony asked the young woman.

"Yes, I do."

"Why do you think so?" Augustus asked, his intelligent blue eyes locked onto Claire.

Claire thought for a few moments. "I don't why. It's a feeling I have."

"That won't hold up in court, my dear," Augustus said.

The corners of the young woman's mouth turned up and she teased the judge. "No? Why not?"

"Does the feeling about the premeditation have any basis in fact?" Augustus questioned. "Perhaps, something you've learned during the interviews has made this seem to be a viable option?"

Claire shrugged. "Maybe I'm wrong. Maybe the suspect took a knife from Janice's kitchen and used it as the murder weapon."

"You may not be wrong because taking a knife from the kitchen may have been preplanned," Augustus pointed out. "The killer may have gone to Janice's house planning to kill her, but didn't want to chance being caught carrying a weapon so decided to use a knife found at the house. Were any knives missing?"

"I haven't heard or read anything about the weapon besides that it was a knife. I don't know where the police think it came from."

"The initial investigation's notes were lost," Augustus said. "Perhaps no one presently in law enforcement knows whether or not a knife was missing from the woman's kitchen. It's a shame the original notes were destroyed. However, as I said, where the murder weapon came from cannot be the determinant for premeditation. The killer could have planned to kill Ms. Carter with a knife he carried with him or with a knife from her own kitchen."

"You're right," Claire said.

"What other reasons might there be for you to suspect premeditation?" Augustus asked.

Taking in a long breath, Claire said, "I think that the actual attack must have been very quick. I know Janice was stabbed many times, but I think the killer did his work quickly because the child in the house didn't wake up. If it was a prolonged attack, the noise in the home would have gone on for some time and the daughter probably would have woken up. But, I guess a fast attack could have been due to rage and not premeditation. The killer might have been set off by something, an argument, being rejected by Janice, who knows?"

"Good points," Augustus told her. "Is there anyone you should interview that you haven't yet?"

"I can't think of anyone."

"Is there anyone you should speak with a second time?"

Claire mentally ran through the interviews

they'd done, but wasn't sure there was a reason to talk to anyone again.

"What about Brandon Willis?" Tony asked. "He was rude and threatening the first time you met with him. Why behave that way? Does he have something to hide?"

Claire's brain went into overdrive. *Does Willis have something he hopes to hide from us?*

"And what about Joe Bricklin?" Tony added. "Maybe he needs to be pressed about why he changed his claim that he saw a man at Janice's door that night."

"Maybe we should re-interview those two," Claire said thoughtfully. "Maybe returning a second time will rattle them and something will slip out."

"Just don't go by yourself when you see those two guys." Tony's face was serious. "If you scare one of them, who knows what he'd do to keep his secret hidden. I doubt he'd hesitate to kill again. Make sure you have Nicole or Detective Gagnon with you. Don't you dare go alone."

The heartfelt warning from the kind store owner warmed Claire's heart.

"If you need me to, Blondie, I'll go along to protect you."

Claire smiled at the man. "Don't be surprised if I take you up on that."

"I'll be ready." Tony went to the storeroom for some supplies and the dogs followed on his heels.

Claire and Augustus walked to the back of the store to the coffee bar where they poured drinks and carried them to the small table.

"I might re-interview Janice's friend, Brittany Patterson. She might be able to shed more light on Joe Bricklin. She was dating him back then. She probably has some good insight about him. I sort of glossed over that when I met with her the first time."

"Whoever you speak with," Augustus said, "remember to be on your guard. The interviewing can set things in motion that you don't expect. Be prepared. Question everything you're told. Trust none of them."

The old judge's warning sent a shiver of alarm down Claire's spine.

18

"I was surprised when you wanted to meet again." Brittany Patterson sat across from Claire and Nicole at a table in a Boston café. "Has something new come up?"

"We're speaking again with everyone we talked to previously," Nicole said. "After talking about the past, we've discovered that people think back and remember things they'd forgotten about."

"Not me." Brittany wore a look of bewilderment that she should have recalled something and hadn't.

"We would like to hear more about Brandon Willis," Claire said. "Can you tell us what his personality was like?"

"We discussed Brandon when you were here

before." Brittany looked at the two young women. "I don't know what else to say about him."

"What did he look like back then?" Claire asked in an encouraging voice.

Brittany frowned and thought for a few minutes. "He had dark hair, brown. He wore it a little longer than other men. He was fairly tall, maybe six feet. Thin. He was good at softball. He always got a hit."

"Would you say he was good looking?"

"I guess you would say that. He wasn't my type though."

"Why not?"

"Like I told you before, he liked to drink too much. He lacked ambition. He didn't seem to have any goals. That wasn't for me. He could be moody, too. He'd turn quiet and sullen. Other times he would talk and make jokes. Too many ups and downs for my taste."

"How was he with women?" Claire asked.

"What do you mean?"

"Was he respectful? Was he always flirting? Did he make inappropriate comments?"

"Hmm. I don't remember him being overly flirty. I don't think I ever heard him make a rude comment."

"Did Brandon get along well with the other guys on the team?" Nicole questioned.

"He seemed to. He was a good player. People wanted him on their team." Brittany took a sip from her drink and pushed a strand of hair over her ear.

"Janice liked him?"

"She was friendly to him. I think she only went out with him a couple of times. I told her he wasn't the right guy for her. She didn't like me voicing my opinions about her dates. I heard she didn't accept his invitations to go out after a couple of dates."

Claire noted the slight change in the information Brittany was sharing. When they'd spoken previously, what she'd told them was a little different.

"Do you know how Brandon reacted to being rebuffed by Janice?"

"I don't," Brittany said. "I'd see him at the games and practices, but we didn't interact much."

"You were dating Joe Bricklin back then," Nicole said.

"That's right."

"Did you date him for a long time?" Nicole asked.

"Not really. A few months. I don't know. Maybe four months or so."

"Why did you stop seeing him?"

"Joe moved away shortly after Janice was killed.

He said he didn't feel safe in the neighborhood. The murder freaked him out. I think he was ready for a change and was probably thinking about moving before Janice died."

"What was Joe like?" Claire asked.

Brittany seemed to be thinking back over the years. "Joe was intelligent, but I don't think he used his brains. He was another guy with no ambition. He was a good athlete, strong, fast."

"What did Joe look like back then?" Nicole asked.

"Joe was thin, but he had strong shoulders. He hard dark eyes, dark hair. He kind of looked like Brandon. People sometimes asked if they were brothers, but I didn't think the resemblance was that strong."

"What was his personality like?"

"Joe wasn't boisterous, but he liked to talk, joke around. He drank, but not heavily. He wasn't much of a conversationalist, really, he only talked about sports, music, celebrities. Joe didn't follow or keep up with current events which I enjoyed. I think you need to be informed and can't put your head in the sand. His conversation was pretty superficial. It was for the best he moved away. We weren't a good match at all. It was easier to just drift apart."

"Did you keep in touch after he moved away?"

"Oh, gosh, no. I was glad it was over," Brittany said.

"Was Joe friendly with Janice?" Claire asked.

Brittany's eyes widened. "He lived across the street from Janice, but I don't think they interacted much. They weren't buddies or anything. Different schedules, different responsibilities." The woman sat up. "Why are you asking about Brandon and Joe? Do you think one of them did something to Janice?"

"We're only gathering as much information as we can," Nicole assured her.

Brittany's voice took on a conspiratorial tone. "I think it was Brandon who tried to snatch that little girl from the ball field. Sometimes his eyes looked really dark, like he was thinking about bad stuff. His moods were unpredictable. Who knows, but maybe he was the one who attacked Janice. Maybe he was angry that she didn't want to date him anymore. What do you think?"

"We just report on our interviews to Detective Gagnon," Claire explained. "We aren't told the details of the investigation. We give him our information and he adds it to the mountain of data that's been gathered." Claire didn't mind not being completely truthful with Brittany about how the investigation worked, and she certainly wasn't going to confide in the woman about who might be guilty.

"Did you happen to see Janice that night?" Claire questioned.

Brittany narrowed her eyes and her voice sounded gravelly. "What do you mean?"

"Did you happen to run into Janice the day she died?"

"No, I didn't," Brittany said. "I wasn't exactly her favorite person at the time."

"You didn't have classes that evening?"

"No, we didn't."

"What did you do that night?" Nicole made sure to keep her voice even.

"I studied. I stayed in. I had a lot to do."

"Had you talked to Janice on the days before the murder?"

"We exchanged pleasantries, but she was still angry at me for giving my opinion on Brandon. Janice didn't want me giving her advice on her love life." Brittany shrugged. "She wouldn't have stayed angry with me. It wasn't that big a deal."

"Did Joe talk to you after Janice got killed?" Claire asked. "Did he mention seeing anyone at Janice's house?"

"Seeing someone there?" Brittany asked.

"Joe told police he might have seen someone at Janice's door that night."

"Really? I didn't know that. He didn't tell me that. Did he say who he thought it was?"

"He only saw a form. He couldn't identify the person."

"Who could it have been?" Brittany asked.

"Joe isn't sure he saw someone. He says now that it might have been a shadow."

"A shadow? He confused a shadow for a real person?" Brittany gaped at the two young women.

"He isn't sure he saw anything."

"Well then, maybe he shouldn't have said anything if he wasn't sure about it." Brittany shook her head. "Joe liked to exaggerate. He told tales. I think he wanted to be important so he would embellish whatever happened to him. I was never sure I could believe what he said. I took everything with a grain of salt. Funny, I'd forgotten that about him." Something passed over the woman's face. "I remember Joe losing his temper a few times. I contradicted something he was embellishing and he did not like that. He raised his voice to me. He told me I didn't know what I was talking about. Joe was almost menacing. His face got all contorted. I thought he might hit me."

The little hairs on the back of Claire's neck stood up. "This happened only once?"

Brittany said, "Twice, I think. I didn't like it. I told Joe never to do that to me again."

"How did he take that?"

"I didn't confront him in the middle of his hissy fit. I talked to him about it the next day. I wouldn't have said anything when he was so angry. I was afraid he would strike out. He grumped at me when I told him I wouldn't tolerate that kind of behavior."

Nicole asked, "Did you ever see Joe in an argument with one of the softball players? Did he ever get into a fight?"

"Not that I saw," Brittany said. "That doesn't mean it didn't happen though."

"You look very athletic," Claire noted. "Do you run?"

"I work out all the time. I lift, run, bike. I like to keep fit."

"Were you involved in athletics when you were younger?"

"No, I wasn't. I got involved after Janice died. Maybe it was my subconscious telling me if I didn't want to end up like Janice, I'd better be strong." Brittany's eyes darkened. "Unexpected things have unexpected consequences. I think about the night Janice died. If we hadn't got into a snit about me criticizing Brandon, I might have been at Janice's house that night. We often studied together. We'd put the television on as background noise and then we'd quiz each other or go over lab notes. I could have been there. I might have been killed, too." Brittany's shoulders gave a little shake. "Fate. Fortune's favors. Some people are lucky ... and some are not."

19

Claire returned to the townhouse after a run with Ian, showered, and made a personal pan pizza for herself after feeding the two dogs their dinner. Ian had to work a night shift so he wasn't available to stay for dinner. The chilly October air kept Claire inside and she took her pizza to the living room, made a fire in the fireplace, and put on some music before settling onto the sofa with a cozy blanket.

Despite wanting an evening free of the cold case, she couldn't stop bits and pieces of conversations she'd had and details she'd read from old news accounts and the retired officer's report on the murder from swirling around and around in her head. Setting her dinner plate on the coffee table,

Claire sighed. "I can't escape it," she told the Corgis and got up to get her own notes on the case from her desk.

There were things that bothered her after speaking the second time with Brittany Patterson, but try as she might to understand the reason for her concerns, she couldn't place why things felt off when she'd talked with the woman. Thoughts and ideas seemed to flit by invisibly on the air, but Claire was unable to grasp at them.

Flipping through her case notes, her phone buzzed. Tessa wanted to come by. She had a friend she wanted to introduce to Claire.

Twenty minutes later, Claire met the two women at her front door and invited them to come in and sit by the fire.

Bear and Lady welcomed the visitors with wiggles and wagging tails.

Tessa's friend, Rowan Mink, was a few inches taller than Claire, willowy, with long brown hair that hit past her shoulders, and the brightest blue eyes Claire had ever seen. It was hard to judge the woman's age. Claire initially thought Rowan was in her early thirties, but the more she looked at her, the less sure she was about her guess.

"What a wonderful fire." Before taking a seat,

Rowan held her hands out to the flames for their warmth.

"It's a chilly night." Tessa shivered and sank onto one of the comfy white chairs that flanked the fireplace. "The fire is just what I needed."

Claire brought out tea and a plate of cookies and the three women engaged in pleasant chit-chat about the weather, the fall season in Boston, and their various travels to different places around the world.

Rowan set her teacup on its saucer. "Tessa tells me you're having some difficulty with a cold case."

Claire almost spit out her mouthful of tea. She gave Tessa a quick look of surprise. "I ... yes, it's a bit of a mess at the moment."

Rowan leaned forward. "Do you feel things on the air?"

Dumbfounded, Claire's mouth dropped open slightly.

Tessa said, "Rowan knows about your skills. She has abilities of her own."

"Are you from Boston?" Claire wondered why Tessa had never introduced Rowan to her before.

"I live in London right now," Rowan explained with a smile. "I met Tessa years ago. We help each other out."

"Are you here for a visit?" Claire asked.

"Just passing through," Rowan said. "I understand your skills are new to you, but Tessa told me you're doing quite well becoming accustomed to them."

Claire let out something that was halfway between a gasp and a laugh. "I don't know if I'd agree with Tessa's assessment."

"Tell me how you think things are going." Rowan's voice was warm and soothing.

Claire took in a long breath. "About a year ago, I started to pick up on people and situations, almost like I had a hyper-focused intuition. I'd know things before they happened, I could sometimes sense danger, I knew things that other people didn't. I had no idea what was going on. My friend, Nicole, and I were standing on a corner of a Boston street one night when a terrible feeling of foreboding came over me. I grabbed Nicole and pulled her to the ground. A car sped by and gunshots rang out. We would have been hit if we hadn't hit the sidewalk."

Rowan held her teacup in one hand and nodded. "Something similar happened to me. I was very young when I experienced a burning sensation of peril. Paranormal things run in my family so it wasn't as unexpected or frightening for me."

"Nicole and I were sort of pulled into a murder case right after we almost got shot," Claire said. "My intuition helped solved it."

"Tessa tells me it is inconsistent for you. That it is maddening when you need the skill and it doesn't come through," Rowan said.

"That's right. Often when I need it most, my skill vanishes." Claire looked down at her hands. "There are times when I wish it would go away and leave me the normal way I used to be, but then when the skill goes dead on me, I'm afraid it won't ever come back." Claire gave a weak smile. "I guess I'm very wishy-washy."

Rowan chuckled. "Not at all. What you're going through is actually quite normal. At least for those new to the special experiences. Things will settle down. You'll learn to control your abilities. There are times when you don't want to know things about people, you don't want your skills intruding. You will learn to turn them off when you don't want to discover things about others and you will learn to turn them on when you need help with something."

"How long does that take?" Claire asked. "When will I be able to do that?"

Rowan tilted her head thoughtfully. "It can take years."

Claire's shoulders sank. "Years?"

"Don't be discouraged. Over the years, you begin to gain control a little at a time. You'll notice it. Each year, you will see improvements in what you can do."

"Do you have a similar ability to mine?" Claire asked.

"I'm able to sense danger and pick up on things about people and situations like you do," Rowan said.

Tessa glanced at Rowan and then turned to Claire. "Rowan is well-respected in the paranormal world. She is well-known all over the world. We're lucky to have her here with us this evening."

Claire stared at Tessa and then turned her eyes to Rowan.

"Is there anything you'd like to ask me?" Rowan said.

Giving a shrug and raising her hands in a helpless gesture, Claire deadpanned, "Can you solve this case I'm on?"

Rowan laughed. "I only have limited time in Boston, so no, I'm sorry, I can't."

With a sigh, Claire nodded.

"But...."

One of Claire's eyebrows raised hopefully.

"I might be able to help you get better in touch with your own skills."

The Corgis jumped up from their places on the area rug and let out yips.

"How?" Claire asked eagerly.

"In just about everything, we are stronger together," Rowan said. "We gain strength from being with one another. Together in understanding, our power grows."

"Just being with you and Tessa will help me?"

"Yes, but there is something simple we can do that may help you better access your abilities." In a graceful motion, Rowan stood up from her chair. "Would you like to try?"

Claire shrank back slightly against the sofa. "Will it hurt?"

Rowan's laugh was like shining silver. "It won't hurt at all." The woman held out her hand to Claire. "Come on. We'll stand in front of the fire. The warmth of the flames will help us."

The dogs moved closer to watch as Claire stood hesitantly and then walked over to stand next to the mysterious woman.

"Tessa, would you please dim the lights and come join us?" Rowan asked.

Tessa did as she was asked and moved to Claire's side.

"We will form a half-circle," Rowan explained and took hold of Claire's hand.

Tessa held Claire's other hand and the three faced the fire.

Rowan began to mutter in a language Claire could not place and as it continued, Claire watched the woman out of the corner of her eye.

The flames in the fireplace suddenly roared and flared causing Claire to startle and when she almost stepped back, Rowan held tightly to her hand encouraging her to stand her ground.

The heat of the dancing flames commanded Claire's attention and the young woman felt compelled to keep her eyes pinned on the fire. Feeling her muscles begin to relax, her worries and tensions began to melt away. A sensation of peace and calm filled her heart.

Claire imagined red doves emerging from the fire, slowly flying into the air, losing their crimson color, and turning brilliant white. The birds moved slowly around her in a graceful, mesmerizing circle.

The Corgis sat quietly, watching the white doves glide gently on the air.

Feeling as though she was about to leave the

floor and rise up, Claire breathed deeply and felt her worries fall away and her spirits soar like the birds.

Rowan's voice spoke softly in Claire's mind.

Let what you can do go free and fly like the doves. Let what you can see and feel be part of you. Everything you need is available to you. Let it flow over your hands like water.

Claire's eyelids closed and she fell back easily and unencumbered.

When her lids fluttered open, Claire found herself on the sofa covered with a blanket and the dogs asleep on the floor next to the couch. The fire had died out and a chill floated on the air.

Tessa and Rowan were gone.

Claire moved her hand over her forehead.

Had the women really visited her ... or had she only dreamt it?

20

Under the overcast, late afternoon sky, Claire and Nicole waited in the parking lot of an automotive repair shop and when they saw the man come out and head to his car, they got out of their rented vehicle and walked across the gravel lot towards him.

The man gave them a quick look and glanced away, but recognition dawned and he turned and faced the young women with an unwelcome stare.

"What do you two want?" Brandon Willis asked with a trace of a growl. His dark chinos were grease-stained and his blue work shirt had a smudge of oil on the sleeve. "I already said all I had to say."

Ignoring the man's comment and with her blond

curls moving around her shoulders from a chilly breeze, Claire asked, "Do you have a few minutes?"

Willis was about to say no, but Nicole headed him off. "We could buy you a coffee and a sandwich." She smiled and gestured across the street to a diner. "I promise we won't take much of your time."

Looking over at his car and then flicking his eyes to the diner, Willis sighed. "Fine."

Settling into a booth, the women ordered coffee and slices of pie and Willis ordered coffee and a burger.

"Why are you back to bother me?" Willis demanded. "I answered all your questions last time."

"We'd just like to talk a little more," Claire said. "We're speaking again with everyone we interviewed previously."

"Why?" Willis wrapped his hand around his mug.

Claire said, "Sometimes when people think about the past, new things come up. It might not seem important, but when added to the stack of information, it could be the one thing that tips the balance."

"I got nothing more to add." Willis swallowed some of his coffee.

"Could you tell us about Joe Bricklin?" Claire asked.

"What about him?" Willis narrowed his eyes.

"What he was like," Nicole said. "You and he played on the same softball team?"

"Yeah, we did."

"Did you get along with Joe?"

"Why wouldn't I?"

"What was he like?" Nicole repeated the question.

Willis shrugged. "A regular guy. We all horsed around. We got together to practice."

"Was he quiet? A jokester?"

"Neither. He went along with the group."

"Did he drink a lot?"

"I don't know. He had a few beers when the rest of us did."

"Was he a good athlete? Was he good at softball?"

"Yeah, he was. What's that got to do with the woman's murder?"

"We're just trying to get a better picture of the people around Janice," Claire said.

"He wasn't around Janice," Willis told them.

"Joe Bricklin lived across the street from Janice," Nicole said. "They were neighbors."

"Neighbors?" Willis's eyes widened. "I didn't know that. You sure?"

"Yes," Claire said. "We're sure."

Willis said, "Huh," and scratched his head. "You think Bricklin had something to do with Janice's death?"

"We don't have any evidence that points to that," Claire said. "Mr. Bricklin is just someone who was around her."

"Have you talked to him?" Willis questioned.

"We met with him once," Nicole said. "We plan to speak with him again soon."

"What did he say? Did he seem suspicious?"

Claire sat straighter. "No one stands out as suspicious at this time."

"I can't see Bricklin as a killer." Willis shook his head.

"Why do you say that?" Nicole asked.

"He wasn't aggressive or nothing."

"Did you ever see him angry? Did you ever see him lose his temper?"

"I don't think so. He seemed sort of laid back. I don't see him attacking a woman."

"Did you know Bricklin pretty well?" Claire asked.

"Not very, I guess, but wouldn't you notice something in the guy if he could kill a person?"

"Not always," Nicole said. "Unfortunately."

Brandon Willis's discussion of his former teammate sounded to Claire like the considerations of an innocent man. The way he talked about Bricklin ... the way he talked about expecting to see a trace of menace or strangeness in a potential killer didn't sound like something a guilty person would bring up. If Willis was Janice's attacker, why wouldn't he try to plant a seed about Bricklin being the killer to remove attention from himself?

Willis had been accused of an attempted abduction of a child and had been released because there was no evidence to back up the Harrison children's claim that he was the man near the basketball courts that night so long ago. Had he done it? Had Willis knocked Sally Harrison from her bicycle? Did he run away and end up at Janice Carter's front door? Did he kill her?

Claire stifled a sigh of frustration. Why wasn't her sixth sense kicking in? Why wasn't her skill helping her to figure this out? She looked into Willis's eyes to search for a darkness lurking within, but she couldn't find it. Was it not there? Was he hiding it?

"You mentioned that all the ball players were given orange hoodies," Claire said.

Willis gave her a questioning look. "Yeah. So?"

Claire asked another question. "Was there anyone on your team who seemed off?"

"Off? You mean like a killer?" Willis asked.

"Like someone with anger simmering inside him. Someone who seemed like a loner. Maybe not too friendly, kept to himself."

The waiter brought the pie slices for the women and the burger for Willis.

"I don't know. I didn't notice anyone who seemed like an angry person." The man picked up his hamburger and then paused.

"Was there anyone hanging around to watch the games who might have seemed off? Maybe a buddy of one of the players?"

"I remember one guy, a friend of Joe Bricklin, who came to a lot of games. He was real quiet. He didn't seem off though. There didn't seem to be anything wrong with him."

"Who was he?" Nicole asked.

"Bricklin's roommate."

"Bricklin had a roommate?" Claire asked.

"Yeah, he did."

"Do you remember his name?"

Willis leaned back in his chair in thought. "Let's see. He had kind of a funny name. What was it?" Willis's eyes brightened. "It was Doug. Doug Duggin. We called him DD. It's a weird name, isn't it?"

"It's different," Nicole agreed.

"Can you tell us about Doug?" Claire was eager to hear about Bricklin's supposed roommate.

"He was blond. Tall, on the thin side. He didn't play, but seemed to know a lot about baseball, softball. He gave Joe good advice about how to play. DD was a big reason we won so many games."

"Was he friendly?"

"Yeah, just quiet. He seemed like a good guy."

"What did he do for work?" Nicole asked.

"I think he was a plumber," Willis said.

"We heard some people thought you and Bricklin looked like brothers," Claire told the man.

Willis scoffed. "Yeah, they did. I didn't see it. We had the same color hair. We were about the same age. I don't know. Is that enough reason to think we looked alike?"

"Did you and Bricklin hang out together?"

"Only on softball nights."

"Have you talked to Bricklin? Have you seen him at all?"

Willis's eyebrows shot up. "Yeah, like thirty years ago."

"That was the last time you saw him?" Claire asked. "Thirty years ago?"

"Yeah. I moved away. I heard he moved, too. Never saw him again." Willis took another bite of his burger.

"Can you tell us again what you did after leaving the park the night of Janice's murder?" Nicole asked.

Willis wiped his mouth with a napkin and stared at the dark-haired young woman. "I told you what I did."

"Would you mind running through it again?" Nicole smiled at Willis.

"I would mind. Nothing is different. I told you what I did that night."

"You went back into town?" Claire tried to encourage some talk.

"Yeah, I did." Willis's tone was sullen.

"You thought about seeing a movie?"

"I thought about it."

"You changed your mind?"

"That's correct." A touch of sarcasm could be heard in the man's voice.

"What did you do next?"

A faraway look crossed over Willis's face.

"Can you tell us what you did next?" Claire pushed for an answer.

"I just remembered I saw Bricklin in town that night. From a distance. He was with that blond he was dating."

Claire's heart skipped a beat. "The woman who came to your team's games?"

"Yeah. I saw them walking down the street."

"Did you talk to them?"

"No. They were too far away."

"Are you sure it was them?"

A corner of Willis's mouth turned down and he said firmly, "Yeah. I am. I could tell it was them by the way they walked, and Joe had on his orange team hoodie."

"They were headed away from you?"

"Yeah. I saw them about an hour before I wandered over to the ball field."

"You just remembered seeing them?"

"Just now. It popped into my head."

"Are you sure it was the night Janice was killed?"

Willis's eyes held Nicole's with an annoyed stare. "I said it was that night. Do you hear okay?" he sassed her.

"Just checking to be sure." Nicole delivered the words with the same tone of annoyance Willis had used on her.

"After you went back to town, you decided to go for a walk, correct?" Claire tried to turn Willis's attention back to the events of the evening.

Willis's mouth looked tight. "That's what I told you before. Why are you asking me the same questions all over again?"

"In case you recall something new," Claire said. "Like you just remembered seeing Bricklin and his girlfriend in town that night."

"That's nothing important," Willis scoffed.

"You never know," Claire said in an even tone of voice. "Anything can help."

"Well, you know what?" Willis crumpled up his napkin. "I'm done helping. I know what you're trying to do. You get me talking about Bricklin to lower my defenses. You make me think you don't consider me a suspect. It's a trick to catch me off guard. Then you try and get me to slip about something. I'm not having it." Willis stood.

"Do you have something you aren't trying to slip up about?" Nicole asked the man.

"Wouldn't you like to know." Willis grabbed his jacket and headed for the door.

When the café door banged shut, Nicole sighed and looked at Claire. "I guess Mr. Willis doesn't want to talk to us anymore," she said with straight-face.

"I believe you're right," Claire said. "Is it because he has something to hide?"

21

Joe Bricklin's former roommate, Doug Duggin, lived in Jamaica Plain and made his living as a professional plumber. His first name wasn't really Doug. It was Nicolas, but everyone called him by the first syllable of his last name, Dug. The man was in his mid-fifties, his hair was blond, but he was no longer thin. A few extra pounds had found their way onto his frame and he carried it well.

At first, Dug was reluctant to speak with Claire and Nicole saying he had given a statement to police thirty years ago and had nothing more to add. Claire didn't tell him that the case files had been destroyed, instead she told him that since the case was being re-examined, they preferred to hear the details directly from the person who had spoken them. Dug relented and they arranged to meet at a boat house next to Jamaica Pond.

"You used to live in Chatham Village for a while?" Claire asked as they sat inside the boat house near huge windows that looked out over the lake.

"In my mid-twenties. I was just starting out in my career, trying to make a go of it with my own company," Dug said.

"You've done well it seems," Nicole said.

"It's worked out better than I could have hoped." Dug smiled and gave a nod.

"You lived near Janice Carter's house?" Claire asked.

Dug took in a long breath. "Yes, I did. After Janice got killed, I left the house and moved in with my girlfriend. I didn't like living near that place. Every time I passed it, I felt like crying. Honestly, the neighborhood scared me after that. I never felt comfortable. I had to get out."

"You had a roommate?" Nicole asked.

"I did. There were three of us initially, but one guy moved out."

"You didn't look for someone to replace him?"

"We did at first, but then we said what the heck

and didn't bother with it. My roommate had been talking about moving away so we figured we'd wait until the lease was up and then we'd both move on."

"Your roommate's name was Bricklin?" Claire asked.

"That's right. Joe Bricklin."

"How did you know Joe?"

"He worked construction. I was doing the plumbing on a house he was working on. We'd talk, we got to know each other. He was looking for another roommate and I needed to get out of my apartment so it worked out."

"How long did you live together?" Claire asked.

"Two years."

"You knew Joe pretty well?"

Dug smiled. "Well, you know my wife says guys only talk about sports and women and drinking. Maybe she's right. I knew Joe's ways, what he liked to eat and drink, what he liked to watch on television, but I can't really say we actually knew each other all that well. We both worked all day. I was usually with my girlfriend in the evenings. Joe played softball, dated. We didn't run into each other a whole lot."

"Did Joe have a girlfriend?" Nicole questioned.

"He went out with different girls. He had been

dating the same young woman for a while right before we went separate ways."

"Do you recall her name?" Nicole asked.

"Hmm," Dug thought for a few seconds. "Brittany. That's it. It's been a while since I thought back to those days."

"Was it Brittany Patterson?"

"I think that's right. She was blond, thin. She was going to school to be a nurse."

"Did you hang out with Joe and Brittany?"

"No, we'd talk in passing, but we didn't hang out."

"Did you play on the softball team with Joe?"

"Not me, no way," Dug chuckled. "I've always been uncoordinated. I'd rather watch sports than play them. It's safer for me that way."

"What was Joe's personality like?"

"His personality?" Dug shrugged. "A typical guy, I guess. He was easy to get along with as a roommate."

"Did he have a temper?"

"I never saw it if he did."

"Did you know Janice Carter?" Claire watched the man's face.

Dug's shoulders slumped slightly and he shifted his gaze out the window at the lake. "I knew her."

"Would say you were friends?"

"Oh, gosh, no, not friends. Friendly. I mowed her lawn a few times when her regular guy was away. Her kid was a cutie. Poor thing."

"What was Janice like?" Claire asked.

"She was a nice person, always friendly, always a smile. She didn't have it easy, working fulltime, going to school, raising a kid. She worked her butt off, but never once did I ever hear her complain. Her parents were around so that was a help to her. I couldn't believe what happened to her."

"Was your roommate friendly with Janice?"

"Joe liked to talk to her. If she was out in the yard, he'd go over to talk. Like I said, Janice was a real sweetheart. Everyone liked her." Dug's face turned serious with sadness pulling at his facial muscles. "Everyone except for one person, I guess."

"Were you at home on the night Janice died?" Claire asked.

"I was at my girlfriend's place until late. I got home after midnight, maybe closer to 1am. I didn't know anything had happened. The police weren't called until the morning."

"Did the police ask you where you were that night?" Claire asked.

"They sure did," Dug said.

"Did they check with your girlfriend to corroborate that you were there?"

"Yes, they did." Dug smiled. "She's my wife now."

"Joe was at home that night though, is that right?" Nicole questioned.

"I didn't know where he was when I got home. I went right to bed. I didn't know if Joe was home or not ... until later."

"You mean in the morning?"

"No. Joe came home around 4am. I don't know if he'd been drinking, but he was kind of loud. I woke up from him banging around," Dug said.

"Do you know where he was before he got home?"

"I don't. In the morning, he went to work early and I spotted the police when I was heading off for the day. Janice's murder was all anyone talked about."

"Joe told the police he thought he saw someone at Janice's door that night. So he must have been home for part of the evening."

Dug blinked, his face blank. "I didn't know Joe saw someone."

"That's what we read," Nicole said.

"Did what he saw help at all?"

"It didn't. Joe isn't sure now that he saw

anything," Claire told him. "It might have been shadow."

"That's too bad," Dug said shaking his head. "That killer has been walking around free for thirty years."

Something about the conversation picked at Claire. "Joe must have gone out late. Did he often leave the house late at night?"

"Sometimes."

"To see his girlfriend?"

"I suppose. We didn't keep track of each other. We just did our thing."

"Why did you mention that Joe must have been drinking before he came home that night?" Claire asked.

"He was noisy. I woke up. I wanted to use the bathroom, but I had to wait because Joe was showering. When I headed to the bathroom, Joe was in his room stuffing his clothes into a trash bag. I thought he must be drunk."

Claire's head started to buzz and her posture straightened. "Did you ask him why he was throwing out his clothes?"

"He said he got some oil all over them. He was cursing. He was pretty mad."

"Did you ask him anything else?"

"Nope. I used the bathroom and went back to bed."

"Did you ask Joe how he got oil on his clothes?" Claire asked.

"I didn't ask. I didn't really care."

"Did you think it was odd?" Nicole asked.

"Not really. I didn't give it any thought." Dug chuckled. "We were young. We did a lot of dumb things."

Claire's heart pounded. "Did you tell the police about Joe coming home late and throwing out his clothes?"

Dug moved his jaw a little from side to side while he thought. "Maybe? I don't remember talking to them about it, but maybe I did. It was too long ago. I don't remember all the details."

"Was Joe's girlfriend with him when he came home that night?"

"No. He was alone."

Claire's head was spinning and when she didn't ask a follow-up question, Nicole jumped in. "Did you know Brandon Willis?"

Dug made a face. "That was the guy who supposedly attacked a little girl at the ball field beside the basketball courts. He got off. No evidence."

"Did you know him personally? Brandon played on Joe Bricklin's softball team."

"I didn't really know him."

"Did Joe get along with Brandon?"

"I suppose he did. I can't say for sure."

"You knew what Brandon looked like?" Nicole asked.

"Vaguely."

"Did you ever notice him at Janice's house?"

"No. I wouldn't have known it was him if he was there."

"Brandon dated Janice a couple of times. Did Joe ever mention Brandon to you in connection with Janice?"

"I don't think so. If he brought it up, it didn't make an impression on me."

Ten more minutes passed with Nicole finishing up the questioning and then the young women thanked Dug for meeting with them and left the boathouse.

Moving quickly down the sidewalk, Claire was practically shaking. "Why would Joe Bricklin return home late at night and throw out the clothes he was wearing? Why did it have to be done right away? Right then? Why couldn't it have waited until morning?"

Nicole eyed her friend. "Maybe he *was* drunk and was behaving irrationally."

Claire stopped and turned to Nicole. "Or, he was acting completely rationally. Maybe he had to get rid of his clothes because they were covered in blood. Janice's blood."

22

Robby carried a tray of chocolate petit-fours into the walk-in refrigerator and then returned to the marble-top workstation to continue making the sweet creations. "So now you think Joe Bricklin murdered Janice Carter?"

"We aren't sure," Nicole said as she frosted a three-tier vanilla cake. "We should talk to him again."

"Or if he is the killer, you might want to run far, far away from him." Robby used a large knife to cut the cake into small squares.

Claire raised her eyes and stared off. "I had such strange sensations running through my body when Dug Duggin was telling us about Bricklin throwing his clothes into a trash bag."

"What does Clairvoyant Claire think?" Robby asked. "Who's the killer?"

Wiping her hand on a dishtowel, Claire sighed. "I'm not sure yet. But I sure felt weird when I heard about Bricklin's behavior the night of the murder."

"Why would Bricklin want to kill Janice?" Robby asked. "He had a girlfriend, he was friendly with Janice. What was his motivation?"

Nicole dipped her spatula into the bowl of frosting. "How about unrequited love?"

Robby's forehead crinkled. "You think Bricklin was in love with Janice?"

Nicole said, "One of Janice's friends mentioned that Joe would rush over whenever Janice was outside. It sounds to me like Joe was infatuated with Janice, but she wasn't interested in him. Rejected emotions are often a spark to a fire ... a fire of jealousy."

"And rage," Claire agreed.

"What about Brandon Willis?" Robby asked. "He was picked up for an attempt to kidnap a little girl. His plan to abduct the girl was foiled. Maybe in his anger and frustration, he turned to Janice ... and killed her."

"I haven't eliminated Brandon Willis as a

suspect," Claire said as she returned to the whoopee pies she was filling.

"What about the roommate you talked to? Duggin? He lived with Bricklin right across the street from Janice. Why isn't he a suspect?" Robby asked.

"Duggin was with his girlfriend during the time Janice was attacked." Nicole moved the spatula over the cake's third layer spreading the frosting.

"That checks out?" Robby asked with suspicion. "The police know he really was with the girlfriend?"

"It checked out. He was with the girlfriend." Claire nodded.

Robby questioned, "Where did that trash bag of clothes end up?"

"Who knows? It probably got thrown in a dumpster somewhere," Claire said.

"There goes the evidence," Robby sighed. "Lost to the years."

"Along with other evidence that went up in flames in the police station fire decades ago." Claire passed the back of her hand over her forehead. "This case is a mess. So much has been lost. Even if we come up with a suspect, what will be used to tie him to the case? There's no DNA evidence left."

Robby turned around and leaned against the counter with the knife in his hand.

"Put that thing down," Nicole told the young man. "It gives me the creeps when you look at us when you have it in your hand."

Robby narrowed his eyes. "Too menacing for you?" he kidded.

"Don't even joke." Nicole returned to her work.

Robby looked at Claire. "You said there's no DNA evidence?"

"That's right. It was destroyed in the police station fire."

"Well, why don't you tell Detective Gagnon to go get some." Robby cocked his head.

In confusion, Claire and Nicole stared at the young employee.

"What do you mean?" Claire asked.

"Exhume the body." Robby's voice had an edge of excitement to it. "See if any DNA can be extracted from it."

"Can they do that?" Nicole asked.

"Yes, they can." Robby's blue eyes sparkled. "It's been done before. Successfully. Push your detective friend to get on it."

"Why haven't they exhumed the body before now?" Claire questioned.

"To tie the evidence to whom?" Robby asked. "Nothing new has come up before, but now you have the Duggin man telling you Bricklin tossed his clothes in a trash bag a few hours after Janice Carter was killed." Robby narrowed his eyes. "Why was Bricklin in such a hurry to shower when he got home? Why not go to bed for a few hours and shower when you get up to go to work? That guy has 'suspicious' written all over him."

Nicole said, "Maybe that's the reason Bricklin claimed to have seen someone at Janice's front door that night. By claiming someone was at the house you can draw suspicion away from yourself." She looked at Claire. "Are we going to talk to him again? Ask him why he tossed his clothes in such a hurry?"

"I'm not sure," Claire said. "It might be best if Detective Gagnon goes to see Bricklin. We'll explain our thoughts to him when we meet with him tomorrow."

"Ask him about exhuming the body," Robby reminded her. "And you know what? Tell Gagnon to alert the newspapers and news stations. Get a story out there reporting the cold case and the exhumation of the victim's body to access DNA. When the guilty person sees or hears the news, he'll freak. He'll panic. He'll think the police will be closing in on him."

"Who knows what he'll do if he panics?" Nicole asked. "Are we sure we want him to panic?"

"If he panics, he might make a mistake that will cost him," Robby said. "He'll do something that will call attention to himself. Guaranteed."

"Maybe you should abandon your musical career," Nicole suggested. "Maybe you should go into law enforcement."

"My personality is too big for law enforcement," Robby said.

"Putting the story of the exhumation out there is actually a good idea," Claire said.

Robby shook his head and deadpanned, "I have one good idea a couple of times a year."

Claire ignored him.

Nicole said, "We just need to convince Detective Gagnon to have Janice's body exhumed."

"Right," Claire said with a worried expression, but then her face brightened. "If they won't exhume the body, maybe the police can put out a story about how they've managed to get some viable DNA, even though they haven't, in order to try and flush out a suspect. If the killer thinks the police have DNA that can tie him to the crime, then he might make a mistake like Robby suggested."

"It's a game of cat and mouse," Nicole grinned.

"Once the story goes out, the police will have to put officers on our suspects to tail them and wait for the killer to do something dumb."

Robby gently poured ganache over the squares of chocolate cake. "Now that we have the case taken care of, let's talk about another game of cat and mouse."

Claire and Nicole turned to look at the young man.

"What do you have planned for Jim and Jessie from JJ's Bakery," Robby asked. "You're not going to stand for them stealing our shop, are you?"

"There isn't anything we can do to keep them from kicking us out because they negotiated for this space and offered the owner more money to lease it," Nicole said with a frown.

Robby's eyes darkened. "The owner should have given you the opportunity to counter the offer and stay here."

"But, he didn't," Nicole said taking a quick look at Claire. "It is what it is."

"We can't keep the shop in this space," Claire said. "But we might have a surprise for those rats, Jim and Jessie."

Robby rubbed his hands together. "Ooh. Tell me."

"Not yet," Claire said with wink, "but stay tuned. If it works out, I think you're going to like it."

"I bet I'll love it," Robby said. "Jim and Jessie Matthews are monsters. They are so jealous of this store. They're so jealous that we tied for the grand prize at the food festival with them. Like we've said a hundred times, there's more than enough business to go around."

"Some people just don't like strong competitors. They only want the spotlight on themselves. They'll do anything to destroy their competition." Nicole sighed, sad to leave the space she'd turned into one of Boston's hottest sweet shops. "We're going to need some luck, to maintain the shop's success, and to solve this darned cold case."

Claire set her jaw, determined not to allow disappointment to ruin their efforts. She looked from Nicole to Robby. "We're just going to have to make our own luck."

Robby smiled and nodded. "That's my girl."

23

In a black suit, black and white checkered shirt, and a black blazer, Claire walked out of a ten-story building in the city's financial district wearing dark sunglasses. She'd slicked her blond curls back into a bun. Leaving the meeting with her lawyer and her financial advisor, Claire made her way back to Adamsburg Square and entered Tony's market.

"You're looking good, Blondie," Tony told her from behind the deli counter. "But you don't have to dress up to visit me," he kidded.

Bear and Lady heard Claire's voice and ran from the back store room to greet her. Tessa was sitting in back sipping a coffee and Claire went to join her.

"You look very professional today," Tessa smiled.

"You interviewing for a job or something?" Tony asked.

Sitting down at the table with Tessa, Claire shook her head. "I have a job that I love, so no, I wasn't at an interview. But, my meeting did have something to do with the chocolate shop." With a mischievous grin, she added, "You'll have to wait for me to explain in a few days. It's a surprise."

Tony rubbed his hands together. "I love a surprise." He and the dogs headed for the store room.

"I don't like surprises," Tessa said with one eyebrow raised. "Can you let your secret slip?"

"I'd rather not." Claire eyed her friend. "I had a strange dream the other night."

"Oh?" Tessa wrapped her hands around her cup.

"At least, I'm pretty sure it was a dream."

Tessa gave Claire a careful look.

"You came to visit me at home one evening. The fire was going. It was cozy. We talked." Claire sipped her hot tea. "Is your friend, Rowan, in town?"

"Rowan? No, she's not. She's in London. Why do you ask?"

"Rowan was with you. She gave me some advice."

"I see. Then your experience was definitely a dream," Tessa said. "Did the advice help you?"

"I think so. I think it will." Claire shrugged. "But, it was only a dream."

"Don't discount dreams, Claire. They can be very useful." Tessa looked at her friend with a pointed expression. "It can be very hard to send advice through dreams."

A smile slowly spread over Claire's face. "I knew it was more than a dream. Your friend can send messages through a dream, can't she?"

"What a silly notion." The very corner of Tessa's mouth turned up.

"Did you ask Rowan to help me?"

"Hmm, I might have." Tessa checked her watch. "Oh, look at the time. I need to get back to work. I only stopped by for a quick visit with that handsome market owner." Tessa winked and said goodbye. "I'll pop into the back room and grab a kiss from that big lug of mine."

"Tell Rowan thank you," Claire said with a twinkle in her eye.

"I'll do that."

Claire and Tony chatted together for twenty minutes while he worked at the counter when a text came in from Detective Gagnon.

It's happening in a half hour.

"Can the dogs stay here a little longer?" Claire asked Tony. "I need to go to another meeting."

"Those dogs can move in permanently. I'm happy to have their company." Tony carried some paper bags to the front of the store. "You go to your meeting, Blondie. Take all the time you need. We'll be here when you're done."

~

TALL TREES GREW on the far side of the cemetery's property line and their leaves had a soft crimson tinge to them. The late afternoon peacefulness of the place was interrupted by the rumble of a backhoe's engine.

Claire stood off to the side to watch the officials dig into the earth where Janice Carter had been buried. Kelly Carter Cox was next to Claire, sniffing a little and touching a tissue to her eyes.

"Would you rather not watch?" Claire asked kindly. "We can sit in your car."

"I'd rather be here."

The backhoe went silent and several men continued to dig with long-handled shovels. When the casket was raised, it was placed into the back of a hearse and driven away.

When Detective Gagnon approached the women and said kind words of support and encouragement to Kelly, Claire glanced around the area and noticed several people watching the process from different vantage points. They were too far away for her to clearly see their faces, but she felt something like a warning sensation run along her skin.

Before calling a cab to take her back to the city, Claire, along with Detective Gagnon, walked Kelly to her car.

"Now we just have to wait," Kelly said as she gave Claire a parting hug. "I hope they can find some viable DNA. It might be our only hope to solve my mother's case."

"We'll keep our fingers crossed." Claire wasn't pinning her hopes on the examiner's luck extracting DNA from Janice Carter's body. Her real hope was that the exhumation and the subsequent news stories about it would frighten the person responsible for the murder into making a mistake of some kind. Now, it was a waiting game.

Detective Gagnon said, "We gave a good performance to the press. Although we have no idea if viable DNA will be found, we've set the wheels in motion. If the killer thinks we might be on to him, he may do something desperate."

"There's a chance that DNA will be found, isn't there?" Claire asked.

"It's possible to be able to extract Janice's DNA, but the real jackpot will be if the examiner finds foreign DNA on the body that could be matched to the killer. We'll just let our plan for finding foreign DNA on Janice spread through the news agencies and hope that the information reaches the ears of the killer." Gagnon let out a sigh. "It's a heck of a long shot, but at the moment, we don't have much else."

Something pulled at Claire from the right side of the cemetery, but when she turned to look, there was nothing there, but the grassy lawns and the marked graves of the deceased. Giving herself a slight shake, she silently scolded herself for being so jumpy.

"When is Ian returning from the conference?" Gagnon asked.

"Tomorrow. I'm going to pick him up at the airport. He texted and told me it's been a worthwhile event."

"He's lucky he attended a good one," Gagnon said. "They're not all so useful."

The detective asked Claire if she needed a ride

anywhere and when she declined the offer, he headed for his vehicle. "I'll keep you and Nicole in the loop. I'm not going to hold my breath, but with a lot of good fortune, we'll get the break we need in this case."

Claire watched out the window of the cab as it moved along the streets carrying her back to her Boston townhouse. Houses, buildings, trees, a river, the highway all sped past as she traveled.

She thought about Janice Carter, her losses, the vicious end to her life. Who killed her? Why? How did the murderer manage to elude the police for so long? Will it ever be solved? Why can't I do more to help?

Closing her eyes, she rested her head against the vehicle's back seat. The dream she'd had about Tessa and Rowan came into her mind. The fire, the birds, the words Rowan said to her.

Let what you can do go free and fly like the doves. Let what you can see and feel be part of you. Everything you need is available to you. Let it flow over your hands like water.

It didn't feel like her skill was available to her. It felt like it had abandoned her.

How could Rowan send advice to her in a dream?

It seemed so very ridiculous, but the past year

had shown that there were things in the world that could not be explained, at least not by Claire. Paranormal skills, murder, liars, rage and jealousy that could lead someone to kill.

Jim and Jessie Matthews, the bakery owners, who were so envious of and threatened by Nicole that they managed to get her evicted from the building that housed her chocolate shop. How could they even hatch such a mean, hateful, and vengeful plan?

The negative thoughts caused Claire's stomach to ache and she opened her eyes to glance out the window. The cab had stopped at a red light.

Outside was a green park. Some colored leaves blew over the grass. A baby in a stroller was being pushed by his mother. The baby's hat blew off in a gust of wind and bounced quickly away, over the grass. A young man noticed and ran off to capture the little cap. He returned it to the mother with a smile.

The short interaction warmed Claire's heart and lifted her spirits.

Maybe what she needed to do was focus on the good things in the world. Her friends. The chocolate shop. Her Corgis. Tony. Tessa. Robby. Nicole. And, Ian. The joy of her life.

Maybe the power of good was the central point she needed to let her skills fly like the doves in her dream.

A smile played over Claire's lips.

She would grip that power with both hands ... and she would not let it go.

24

On the way home after her shift at the chocolate shop, Claire felt antsy. Before work, she'd met with Detective Gagnon to review the case and discuss where they would go from there. Claire brought up inconsistencies that had been bugging her.

Joe Bricklin made it seem that he hadn't been seriously dating Brittany Patterson, but others reported that the two of them had been a couple. Joe didn't reveal that he went out later in the evening after claiming to see a man on Janice's doorstep. He'd implied that he was home all night. Why did he return to his rented house a couple of hours before dawn in a rush to toss out the clothes he'd been wearing that night?

Brandon Willis claimed to have left the ball field area before the Harrison girl was attacked, but all three siblings were sure it was Brandon who knocked Sally from her bike. Brandon admitted to dating Janice a couple of times, but didn't seem bothered that she didn't want to see him anymore. Was he hiding the fury he'd felt at being dumped? But Brandon supposedly had been stalking Janice.

Brittany Patterson told Claire she'd been at home studying the night Janice was killed, but Brandon remembered seeing her and Joe Bricklin in town together.

Gagnon suggested that Claire talk to Bricklin again about his relationship with Brittany and about where he went later on the night of the murder.

The whole thing picked at Claire. She glanced at the time on her phone and made a decision. Turning around, she headed for the subway to take her to Somerville.

Arriving at Davis Square, Claire checked the notes on her phone to find Joe Bricklin's address, and then walked for fifteen minutes to a neighborhood of tree-lined streets, tended houses, and three decker apartment buildings.

Claire stood in front of Bricklin's small, white ranch-style house thinking she should have called before showing up unannounced at the man's home. She knew Joe got off work at 3pm and might be home by 4 and she was right since his truck was parked in the driveway. Feeling badly about barging in on Bricklin, she decided to walk to the end of the road and give him a call to see if he would be willing to speak with her.

As Claire was about to turn around, a blue truck pulled to the curb and a tall man got out. She noticed a resemblance between this person and Joe Bricklin.

"Excuse me," Claire called.

The man glanced back and looked surprised that Claire was speaking to him. "Me?"

"Yes. Are you Joe's brother, Mack?" Claire introduced herself. "I work with the police as an interviewer. I've spoken with Joe recently."

"Today?" Mack asked. The man had broad shoulders, dark eyes, and dark hair cut close to the head and Claire guessed he must work construction like his younger brother.

"Not today. About a week ago. I need to speak with Joe again, but I didn't make an appointment. I was in the neighborhood," she fibbed, "and thought I'd see if I could catch him at home."

"You said you work for the police?" Mack asked.

"On an as-needed basis, yes."

Mack moved a little closer and took a quick look at Joe's house. "I've been worried about Joe."

A sense of unease raced through Claire. "Have you?"

Mack ran his hand over his head. "Joe seems kind of anxious. He hasn't been himself. He told me the Carter case has been re-opened. It seems to be bothering him."

"Has he said much to you about the case?" Claire asked.

"No, he hasn't. He used to live across the street from the woman. You must know that. I wonder...."

"What? What do you wonder?" Claire's heart began to race.

"I wonder if Joe ... oh, I don't know."

"You have some concerns?"

"Joe seems upset since he found out the case has been opened again." Mack looked to the house again. "Listen, Joe is no killer. He didn't kill that woman, but I wonder ... I wonder if he saw something that night. Something seems to be eating at him."

"Is Joe at home?" Claire asked.

"I came by to pick up a key. Joe told me he's going

away for a few days. He wants me to check on his cat. I had a key, but I can't find it."

Alarm bells rang in Claire's head. "Do you want to talk to Joe about the case? The three of us could sit and talk. Do you think he'd be willing? Do you have the time?"

"Yeah, sure. I think it's best to have Joe get whatever's bothering him off his chest," Mack said. "Maybe if the three of us talk together, he'll open up."

"Does your brother go off for a few days on a regular basis?"

"No, he doesn't. That's why I'm worried that this case is eating at him."

Claire took out her phone. "Let me just text my supervisor and let him know what I'm doing." The message to Detective Gagnon spelled out Mack Bricklin's concerns about his brother and added - *I'm not sure I'm going to go inside. If Joe seems agitated I'm going to leave. If you don't hear from me in five minutes, send help.*

Claire forced a smile. "Okay. Shall we?"

Mack led the way to the front door where he rang the bell.

Claire heard the chimes, but no one answered the door.

Mack hit the bell again. "Joe's truck is here."

"Could he have walked somewhere? Gone for a run?" Claire asked.

"I don't think so." Mack tried the doorknob. Locked. "Let's go around to the back. Maybe he's in the yard."

When they reached the rear of the house, there was no one in the yard. Mack tried the back doorbell, and got the same response. Nothing. Perspiration beaded up on the man's forehead. "I'll call him," Mack said as he removed his phone from his back pocket. No answer.

Mack walked back to the front with Claire right behind and he pressed his face up to the glass in the bay window. His shout sent adrenaline racing through Claire's veins.

"Joe! My brother! He's on the floor!" Mack raced to the front door and crashed against it using his full body weight, but it didn't budge. Hitting the door a few more times produced the same result.

Claire picked up a rock she found next to the driveway and handed it to Mack who used it to break the glass in the door so he could reach inside and unlock the door.

Joe was on the floor of the living room, on his

back, unconscious and all Claire could think about was the image of Janice Carter, dead on her living room floor.

Mack knelt next to his brother and called his name.

Claire saw the blood. Joe's wrists had been slashed. His face was deathly pale.

"He killed himself," Mack wailed.

Claire used her phone to call for an ambulance and then sent a text to Detective Gagnon before kneeling down to check for Joe's pulse. "There's a pulse. He's still alive."

"Joe, Joe," Mack murmured.

Claire noticed the blood pool next to the unconscious man and her heart jumped into her throat. Pulling Joe's shirttail up, she gasped when she saw the knife wound in the man's stomach.

"He didn't try to kill himself." Claire stood, her legs shaking. "Someone attacked him." Wheeling around, Claire listened for footsteps inside the house. Did the attacker run or is he still in the house? She pulled her pepper spray from her small handbag and stood in a defensive posture in case someone rushed them.

Sirens.

Claire breathed a sigh of relief.

In less than three minutes, two EMTs hurried into the room through the front door with a police officer right behind.

Claire gave an account of what had happened when she arrived to the house. Mack was in no state to chime in, he was so distraught about his brother.

Next through the door was Detective Gagnon looking for Claire with nervous eyes. Relief flooded his face when he spotted her standing with the officer.

"Someone attacked him, tried to make it look like Bricklin attempted suicide."

"I suppose Bricklin could have stabbed himself in the stomach before slashing the wrists," Gagnon speculated while taking a look at the man on the stretcher being removed from the house to the ambulance. Mack followed behind to ride with his brother to the hospital.

"No, he didn't," Claire said with authority. "That's what someone wants us to think. We aren't falling for it." She looked Gagnon right in the eyes and lowered her voice. "We wanted to push someone to act with the exhumation of Janice's body. We hoped someone might panic and do something stupid. Well, we got what we wished for, didn't we?" Claire teared up and swallowed hard. "Somebody panicked. Somebody thinks Joe Bricklin knows something important and decided to silence him. Now the question is ... who did it?"

"Any guesses?"

"Brandon Willis?" Claire suggested.

"I'll have someone find out where Mr. Willis was this afternoon. Then I'll pay him a visit and have a talk." Gagnon shook his head. "Bricklin would have bled out if you and his brother didn't show up here."

Claire turned to look at the bloody spot on the wood floor where Joe had fallen.

Her vision dimmed and the image of Janice Carter on the floor of her house swam in her mind.

Janice's hand moved. Her finger touched the pool of blood. She made a letter, and then another one. *B ... R.*

Her finger moved again.

Make the letter, make the next letter, Claire urged. *Tell me who did it. Was it Brandon?*

Janice's finger began to form the next letter.

"Claire? Are you okay?" Gagnon's hand was on her arm.

Claire blinked and when the image of Janice vanished, her heart sank. "I'm okay. I just got a little dizzy," she said softly.

"Let's go outside and get some fresh air." Gagnon maneuvered the young woman to the door.

Before stepping out, Claire took a quick glance back to the blood on the floor.

Almost. So close.

25

Claire paced around the living room of her townhouse, her brain feverishly racing through details and potential clues she'd been able to gather on the case.

Claire wanted to talk the whole thing over with Nicole, but she was on her way to the wedding taste testing with her samples of sweets to try and win the contract to supply the wedding cake and other desserts for the swanky upcoming wedding. The bakers who had been invited for consideration could only bring one twelve-by-twelve-inch platter and all the desserts had to fit on that one tray. Nicole had been a nervous wreck ranting about the requirement that only one baker could attend. "Why can't you two come with me? It's not fair," she'd told Claire and Robby.

"You'll do just fine. You don't need us there," Claire had tried to comfort her friend. "When you win the contract, the three of us will be there at the wedding."

Robby and Claire helped Nicole pack up the goodies and sent her off in a taxi.

Still pacing up and down the length of her living room, Claire was still horrified that someone had tried to murder Joe Bricklin. What does he know? Who attempted to keep him quiet?

Detective Gagnon texted Claire to let her know that Joe was in surgery and it would not be possible to interview him for at least two days.

Claire's brain kept coming back to Dug Duggin's report of Joe tossing out his clothes on the night of Janice's murder. It was not a normal thing to do and it sent up a huge red flag of concern. Joe still could be the killer, but maybe he worked together with someone else to commit the crime and that person decided it would be best if Joe was unable to confess to the murder.

Who was the other person? Decades ago, Joe Bricklin and Brandon Willis played together on the softball team. There was a connection between them, but what could have been their motivation to kill Janice Carter? It wasn't money ... Janice lived paycheck to paycheck.

Bricklin had an infatuation with Janice and Brandon had dated her. From accounts provided in the interviews, it seemed that Janice had rebuffed both men. Were they out for revenge? Did they team up to take revenge on her?

Claire sank onto the sofa with one Corgi on each side of her and she looked at the fireplace. Thinking it would be comforting to light a fire, she dismissed the idea since she had to leave shortly to meet Ian at the airport to welcome him back from the conference he'd attended. She stared at the empty firebox and thoughts of her dream that Rowan was in swirled around in her mind.

Let what you can do go free and fly like the doves, Rowan told her.

There was something important in the message, but what was it?

Letting her head rest against the sofa back, Claire closed her eyes ... and a minute later, a thought flashed into her mind with such force that she sat bolt upright frightening the dogs and causing them to bark.

Brandon Willis told Claire that he'd seen Brittany Patterson and Bricklin, wearing his orange hoodie, walking around town on the night of the attack. Brittany reported to Claire that she'd been at home studying.

A chill squeezed Claire's stomach.

The orange team hoodie.

Brandon Willis, Joe Bricklin, and Brittany Patterson were all close in height. All were slender and fair-skinned.

Claire leaned forward and held her head in her hands. *Oh, gosh. Brittany.*

With her heart racing, she grabbed her phone and called Detective Gagnon.

When he picked up, Claire talked in rapid-fire speech. "I know it's a crazy idea, but I think Brittany Patterson could be the killer. She was dating Joe Bricklin. Maybe she found out Joe had a thing for Janice. Joe thought he saw a man at Janice's door. He retracted his statement. He could have been trying to protect Janice by telling police he saw a man. Joe got home late that night and was tossing out his clothes. He could have been throwing out Brittany's clothes, too. Maybe Joe saw Brittany going into Janice's and went over to see if he could visit with them. But he saw what Brittany did and she forced him to hide her bloody clothes. Joe must have had blood on his own clothes. Maybe Brittany threatened Joe into silence. I don't know, but my intuition is telling me you need to go talk to her. Right now."

Gagnon was quiet on the other end of the call. "It's a possibility."

"Brittany might have attacked Joe today to keep him from telling what he knows. She might be desperate and panicking."

"I'll take a ride over there," Gagnon said. "I'll let you know what I find out."

Feeling slightly better that Gagnon would look into her concerns, Claire ended the call with the detective and then used her phone to order a cab to take her to the airport.

When Claire was ten minutes from Logan Airport, her phone buzzed.

Gagnon spoke. "Brittany Patterson is not at home. Her car is not in the garage and is not in the driveway. Hopefully, she hasn't flown the coop." He said he would put out a bulletin for officers to be on the lookout for her vehicle.

Claire wished him good luck and as soon as she ended the call, her phone buzzed again. This time it was Kelly Carter Cox.

"Claire? It's Kelly. I've been thinking so much about my mother and the crime and the night of the murder. Snippets of things run through my mind ... sights, sounds, flashes of things that happened when I was five. I've been dreaming so vividly, often about waking up in the morning on that terrible day and finding my mother dead on the floor."

"I'm sorry you're reliving it," Claire told the young woman. "I'm so very sorry it happened."

"I want to tell you something. I didn't want to wait until I see you again."

"What is it?" A shiver ran down Claire's spine.

"I've been dreaming the same thing over and over. In the dream, I'm five years old and I'm sleeping in my bedroom on that awful night." Kelly went quiet and Claire waited for her to go on.

After clearing her throat, Kelly said, "I wake up. It's dark. I hear my mother talking to someone in the living room. I hear two women's voices. My mother had a woman visiting that night."

Claire's throat tightened. "This is all in your dream?"

"I remember it whenever I dream about that night," Kelly said. "But the voice ... the woman's voice that I hear ... I'm certain I heard it on the night of the murder."

"Did the woman sound familiar to you?" Claire's hands felt clammy.

Kelly said softly, "I think I heard Brittany Patterson talking to my mother."

Claire tried to keep her tone even. "Do you think it's happening only in the dreams that you recognize the voice or do you think it really happened that night?"

"I think it happened that night," Kelly said. "I think it was Brittany Patterson who was with my mother. In fact, I'd bet anything it was Brittany in our living room."

The image of Janice on the floor of the living room jumped into Claire's head. Janice's finger writing out the letters. B ... R. Was the next letter going to be – I?

Claire could see the airport terminal coming up as the cab headed towards it, and in a few minutes the vehicle pulled to the curb. "I'll tell Detective Gagnon what you remember. It could be very important."

Before ending the call, Kelly said, "I know Joe Bricklin was attacked earlier today. Someone tried to kill him. Be careful, Claire."

Ice cold fear rolled through Claire's body. If Brittany killed Janice and attacked Bricklin that very afternoon, she must be in a desperate state. She must be willing to do whatever is necessary not to be taken into custody.

Claire wanted to run into the terminal, wrap her arms around Ian, and go home as quickly as they could.

With her heart beating like a bass drum, Claire headed into the busy terminal that buzzed with activity. After checking the flight board to be sure Ian's plane was on time, she started walking to his gate.

A sense of panic rushed over Claire and she stopped. Rowan's words played in her mind again. *Let what you can do go free and fly like the doves.*

Fly like the doves.

Fly.

Brittany is going to try to the flee the country.

Claire's head whipped to right and she studied a group of people moving through the airport. Most of them pulled small, wheeled, carry-on bags behind them. Something caught her eye.

A bright red scarf with colorful geometric patterns on it.

The scarf was around the neck of a woman with blond hair wearing an expensive light jacket and black boots. The woman was in her late fifties or early sixties.

Brittany.

A gasp escaped Claire's throat as she shook her shoulders and forced herself to follow the woman to keep her in her sights.

She made a call to Detective Gagnon. "I see Brittany. I'm at the airport. She's right ahead of me. She must be trying to leave the country."

"Keep a safe distance from her," Gagnon was almost shouting. He asked what terminal she was in. "Don't approach her. Don't let her notice you. I'm going to hang up so I can call airport security. I'll also send some officers. She needs to come in for questioning. Do not put yourself in danger. I'll call you back in a few minutes."

Claire hurried her steps. She couldn't lose sight of the woman.

Brittany. The killer.

You aren't about to fly out of here. The police will be here soon. Your time is up. It's the end of the line for you.

26

Claire lost the blond woman in a crowd heading to the security line and she panicked for a moment until she caught sight of the back of Brittany's head. Bobbing and weaving through the terminal, Claire's heart thudded with nervousness. *What should I do if she gets into the security line? What should I do if she leaves the terminal?*

When Brittany bent to remove something from the front pocket of her small suitcase, she noticed Claire in the distance. She locked eyes with her.

Brittany crumpled what she'd taken out of the suitcase and shoved it into the pocket of her light jacket. Claire gave a forced smile and a wave, trying to seem that nothing was wrong and that she was pleasantly surprised to run into the woman at the airport.

Claire's smile didn't work.

Brittany whirled around and moved quickly away.

Glancing around the space for an officer or a security guard, Claire moved forward without finding anyone who might be able to help her.

Brittany ducked outside and hurriedly crossed four lanes busy with vehicles coming and going from the terminals. Claire spotted her deft maneuver at the last second and darted out the wide glass doors to keep the woman in her sights.

"Brittany," she called trying to make it seem she was only interested in saying hello, but the blonde walked as fast as she could in the opposite direction.

Taking a quick look over her shoulder, Brittany rounded a corner, abandoned her suitcase, and began to jog.

Claire made the turn, but could not see where the woman had gone so she stood in one place and turned around in a circle searching for her.

A sign for the restrooms pointed down a long hall and Claire made the spilt-second decision to head that way. She broke into a jog and raced to the women's room where she burst through the door and stood askance.

Walking slowly up and down, she trained her gaze below the stall doors for black booted feet.

Nothing.

With a sigh, Claire walked to the exit and was about to turn into the hallway, when a hand settled heavily on her shoulder, something hard was jabbed into the side of her waist, and a woman whispered close to her ear.

"If you value your life, keep a serene look plastered on your face and move in the direction I'm guiding you."

Claire played dumb, but allowed the woman to move her along. "What are you doing? What are you up to? Why are you acting this way?"

"Don't ask stupid questions," Brittany's voice sounded like she had a mouth full of gravel. "You know what's going on." She gave Claire a slight shove. "You're a smart woman. It was only a matter of time." An iron grip squeezed Claire's arm. "I need to get out of here and you aren't going to get in my way."

Brittany's fingers dug into Claire's arm and she directed the young woman through the doors into the parking garage where she found the elevator, pushed the up button, and dragged Claire inside when the doors opened.

"We're going for a little ride." Brittany punched the button for the fifth floor.

"I'm not going anywhere with you." Claire snarled.

A harsh smile gave Brittany's face an ugly appearance. "Too late. You have no choice."

The elevator lurched to a stop and when the doors opened, Brittany said, "Move to the back of the elevator car. Do it," she screamed.

Claire took a step back.

"Stay there and don't move. Better yet, kneel down and put your hands behind your head."

"No." Claire was certain that Brittany would try to stab her or shoot her when she was in a vulnerable position and unable to defend herself.

Brittany had her hand against the elevator door to keep it from closing. "Kneel," she shrieked.

"Keep yelling," Claire told the woman with a sneer. "Someone will hear you and come to see what's going on."

"Shut up. Turn around and kneel."

Claire wouldn't budge thinking if Brittany had a weapon in her possession, she would have used it by now. She took slow steps forward, advancing on her.

The woman's face turned stony and she lunged at Claire, cursing.

Claire raised a hand, clasped it into a fist, and pounded Brittany right in the face just as the elevator door closed with the two women inside and began its slow descent to a lower floor.

Brittany caught Claire under the chin with a strong blow sending her staggering back, sparks flaring in her brain and light-headedness causing her head to spin.

When Brittany came at her again, Claire side-stepped her, wheeled and punched again, this time, the blow landing against the woman's shoulder.

With sweat running down the side of her face, Claire crouched, her fists up, ready to continue the battle.

When the elevator door opened on the first floor, Brittany bolted to escape, but Claire was too quick. In a split-second, she extended her leg catching the woman's foot and sending her flying out onto the hard tiled floor of the terminal. Losing her balance in the melee, Claire tumbled forward and hit the floor right behind Brittany and scrambled forward before her opponent could get up.

Claire sat on the woman and pulled both of Brittany's arms behind her back until the blonde wailed in pain.

Four businessmen stood to the side, their mouths open and eyes wide, staring at the surprising scene before them.

"Get security," Claire bellowed. "Now."

~

Sitting in an airport security office holding an ice pack to her swelling lip, with her hair askew and her jacket ripped, Claire had done her best to explain what had happened and that Brittany Patterson was wanted by the police.

Detective Gagnon and several other officers finally arrived and took Brittany into custody for assault and battery and would have a long talk with her about a crime that had been committed thirty years ago. The woman was hauled off by two officers.

Gagnon asked questions and Claire answered as best she could.

"I didn't say a word to Brittany about being a suspect in Janice Carter's murder. I figured I'd leave that to you." When Claire smiled, she winced from the discomfort of her broken lip.

"I didn't know you could throw a punch," Gagnon smirked.

"Neither did I." Claire gingerly rubbed the side of her face.

When Ian's flight landed, a security guard was there to meet him and led him to the office where Gagnon and Claire were waiting.

When Ian came in through the door, he stopped short for a moment when he saw his girlfriend battered and bruised, his eyes wide with worry. "Are you okay?" He rushed to Claire's side and hugged her gently. "Is anything broken?"

"I don't think so even though my nose was bleeding for about twenty minutes. Sorry I wasn't at the gate to meet you." Claire's jaw ached like crazy from taking a blow.

Ian knelt next to Claire's chair and smiled at her. "You did a good job."

Gagnon cleared his throat. "A word of warning. Never make this woman angry."

Ian laughed. "I'll always stand an arm's length away." He pulled his girlfriend close and ran his hand over her long blond curls. "Forget that idea. That's never going to work."

Claire attempted a chuckle and groaned. "I think

maybe I should go to the hospital to get checked out now. I wanted to wait for you."

Ian helped her to her feet. "Come on, hon. And when we're done there, I'll take you home and make you some tea. Then I'll give you your pain meds and help you to bed."

Feeling safe and loved in Ian's care, Claire slipped her arm through his and let him lead her aching body slowly outside to get a cab.

27

Brittany Patterson was arrested for the murder of Janice Carter. Joe Bricklin came out of his surgery with a request to speak to the police. When Detective Gagnon arrived in his hospital room, the man spoke nonstop for an hour and when the nurse reminded them that Joe needed to rest, law enforcement returned the next day to hear the rest of the story.

Joe did see someone at Janice's door on the night of the murder. It was his then-girlfriend, Brittany. He decided to go over to join the women, but when he crossed the street, he heard what sounded like a fight inside the house.

When he reached for the door knob, the door

flew open and Brittany practically knocked Joe off the front steps in her haste to escape.

Joe sobbed when he told Gagnon what he saw that night. Janice was dead on the floor from knife wounds inflicted by Brittany Patterson.

Brittany threatened Joe into silence. She said she would kill Joe if he told, but before she killed Joe, she would murder Joe's brother ... while she made Joe watch.

Joe said, "She screamed at me, waved that bloody knife right in my face. I've never seen anyone so crazed. She scared me to death so I did what she asked. I took her clothes and my clothes and stuffed them into a garbage bag. The next morning, I drove fifty miles out of my way to dispose of the garments. I wanted her to get caught. I prayed she would. I told the police I saw someone at Janice's door, but in my nervousness, I stupidly said I saw a *man*."

When Joe was asked if he and Brittany were in town walking around together the night of the murder, Joe replied, "We went out for dinner and then we walked around town for a little while. I was tired from a long work week and Brittany told me she needed to study. Before we split up and said goodbye, we had a fight. Brittany accused me of flirting with Janice, of having the hots for her. I did, but I denied it. I only said I thought Janice was pretty and fun... well, Brittany went ballistic. She said she'd never go out with me again, we were finished. She actually punched me in the face."

Claire had come up with the idea that Brittany had planned to kill Janice before she arrived at the bungalow. Claire also had another idea.

When Joe was asked if he was wearing his orange softball hoodie that night, Joe told the police he had been wearing it until Brittany got cold. Then he gave it to her to wear.

Claire thought that Brittany must have headed to the ball field on the way home and when she noticed Brandon Willis sitting in the park and the kids playing there, she devised a second plan. She would set up Brandon as the perpetrator in two incidents that would happen that evening.

Brittany knocked Sally Harrison from her bike and menaced the child before running off hoping to implicate Brandon as the attempted abductor. Claire surmised that Brittany tightened the hoodie around her face and put on sunglasses.

The attack on the child was quick. Brittany and Brandon were similar in height and build. It would be easy for the child to accuse Brandon Willis because he was seen at the park right before the attack.

Not only did Brittany hope Brandon would become a suspect in the abduction attempt, but that he might also be suspected of killing Janice Carter.

In a town where nothing ever happened, two terrible events on the same night would have to be linked, wouldn't they, Brittany must have thought.

Hopefully, the full truth would eventually come out at the woman's murder trial.

∽

Claire, Nicole, and Robby bustled around the chocolate shop preparing for the morning rush.

"When are you going to find out if you won the test taste and will get the contract to cater that wedding?" Robby put the finishing touches on a tray of chocolate and vanilla custards.

"In a couple of days," Nicole said. "I was a nervous wreck at the taste test. I could barely string a sentence together. I'm sure they thought something was wrong with me."

"At least you didn't faint like you did at the food festival," Robby grinned. "That was really something."

Claire peeked into the back room. "They're coming."

"Who?" Robby asked.

Nicole stood straight and adjusted her apron. "Come out front and see." She smiled as she left the work room and headed for the front of the shop.

Claire and Nicole pretended to busy themselves as the door opened and in came the property manager and two other people. Jim and Jessie Matthews of J J's Bakery, the ones who negotiated with the building's owner to pay more for the lease in order to have Nicole kicked out.

The property manager said, "This is Claire Rollins and Nicole Summers."

"We know who they are," Jim Matthews said with a distasteful tone to his voice.

"Well. Good." The manager stammered. "Ms. Rollins and Ms. Summers have recently purchased the building."

Jessie Matthews glared at the manager. "*This* building?"

The manager said, "Ms. Rollins and Ms. Summers have agreed to honor your lease. However, if you would prefer to break the lease and not rent the space from them, they will allow you out of the contract."

Jim and Jessie became red-faced and blustered words to the effect of how could this happen and why weren't they informed, to which the property manager only shook his head and shrugged.

"We're breaking the lease," Jim Matthews announced with angry eyes and a loud voice.

He and Jessie stormed out of the building.

Watching from the doorway to the work room, Robby whooped with joy at the unexpected turn of events.

"And don't let the door hit you on the way out," Nicole muttered to the Matthews, her arms crossed over her chest.

Claire turned to Robby. "The store next door is closing. The owner is retiring. We're going to take over that space, too. It's time for Nicole to expand."

"Oh, happy day," Robby began to sing in his most entertaining way as he high-fived Nicole and Claire. "Onward and upward, my two crazy co-workers."

"You mean your two crazy *bosses*," Nicole corrected.

"Same thing," Robby winked. "When am I being brought in as the third partner?"

"Don't hold your breath," Nicole bopped the young man playfully on the arm.

As the three of them headed to the back room to

finish the morning prep, Robby said, "I will never, for as long as I live, forget the look on Jim and Jessie's faces. They couldn't get out of here fast enough. Well done, you two. Well done."

∽

CLAIRE AND IAN each held one of the Corgi's leashes as they strolled along the river on the cold, late October afternoon under the red, orange, and yellow leaves of the tall trees lining the path. Every now and then, Bear and Lady stopped to sniff at spots on the trail.

"It will be Halloween soon," Claire said with a smile as her feet rustled over some fallen leaves. "I love Halloween."

"Me, too," Ian admitted. "The costumes, the candy, the little kids all excited." With a grin he added, "The candy."

"You said that twice," Claire told him.

"I thought it should be emphasized. You know I have a sweet tooth."

"It's a good thing you work out all the time … otherwise…."

"You wouldn't like me if I wasn't in shape?"

"I'd have to think about that," Claire teased.

After walking further down the path, Claire took Ian's hand. "I have something else I need to tell you."

Ian eyed her. "What could you possibly have left out of the last chat we had? You've already told me you worked as a lawyer, you were married previously, and that you have paranormal skills. What's next? You're really an alien?"

"Not quite." Claire chuckled. "When my first husband passed away, he left me some money."

"That's great," Ian said.

"There's more to it than that."

"How so?"

Claire stopped walking. "Nicole and I didn't need to take a loan to buy the North End building. I paid cash."

Ian's eyebrow went up. "That building is worth a lot of money."

"I have a lot of money." Claire stepped closer to Ian and whispered in his ear to tell him how much she was worth.

Ian's eyes nearly popped out of his head as he staggered back two steps with his mouth hanging open.

"Do you only like me for my money?" Claire asked him.

When he found his voice again, Ian cleared his

throat and smiled. "Well, now that I know how wealthy you are, maybe that has become half the reason I like you."

"What's the reason for the other half?" Claire grinned and narrowed her eyes. "My paranormal skills?"

"I always knew you had those extrasensory-type of skills."

"Did you?" Claire asked in surprise.

"Yeah," Ian tugged her close. "I knew as soon as you put that spell on me. The spell that made me fall head-over-heels in love with you."

With the Corgis bouncing around them and barking their approval, Claire took Ian's face gently in her hands, and just before she leaned in to kiss him, she said, "Then you must have paranormal skills, too. Because you've cast that very same spell over me."

And when Claire stepped closer and pressed her lips against Ian's, somehow it just didn't seem quite as cold out anymore.

THANK YOU FOR READING!

Books by J.A. WHITING can be found here:
www.amazon.com/author/jawhiting

To hear about new books and book sales, please sign up for my mailing list at:
www.jawhitingbooks.com

Your email will never be sold, shared, or spammed.

If you enjoyed the book, please consider leaving a review. A few words are all that's needed. It would be very much appreciated.

BOOKS/SERIES BY J. A. WHITING

*CLAIRE ROLLINS COZY MYSTERY SERIES

*PAXTON PARK COZY MYSTERIES

*LIN COFFIN COZY MYSTERY SERIES

*SWEET COVE COZY MYSTERY SERIES

*OLIVIA MILLER MYSTERY-THRILLER SERIES
(not cozy)

ABOUT THE AUTHOR

J.A. Whiting lives with her family in New England. Whiting loves reading and writing mystery stories.

Visit / follow me at:
www.jawhitingbooks.com/
www.bookbub.com/authors/j-a-whiting
www.amazon.com/author/jawhiting
www.facebook.com/jawhitingauthor

Made in United States
Troutdale, OR
07/05/2023